Lessons Learned the Hard Way:

16 Things Every Teacher Should Know

Lessons Learned the Hard Way:

16 Things Every Teacher Should Know

Bill Hoatson

To order additional copies of this book, contact:
Xlibris LLC
1-888-795-4274
www.Xlibris.com
Orders@Xlibris.com
603375

Books by Bill Hoatson:

Mr. Harrison's Classroom: A Documentary

Lessons Learned the Hard Way: 16 Things Every Teacher
Should Know

Second Period at the Center

Professor Johnson Unhinged: Lectures on Teaching and
Parenting.

Visit www. childachievement.com

CONTENTS

Introduction

Before we begin, let me address the style of my so-called writing. I am not a writer, per se. I am a lecturer. I talk a lot. I have had decades of talking in schools to students, parents and teachers in an attempt to share what I consider valuable ideas on creating successful children. So, what you have here is a long talk, which is different than a book, which is driving my editor crazy because he thinks that he is dealing with a proper piece of writing. Any and all pretense of real writing and its restricting rules don't apply to a lecture, thank goodness, and let's said editor off the hook. So, let's talk.

Part One:
Outside the Classroom

Forces at play on the Child

"All men are created equal," is a cornerstone of our wonderful democracy. Unfortunately, the powers that be, which is everybody BUT the teacher, seems to think that this adage applies to children, which is absurd. All children are not created equal. All children are not raised equal. All children do not learn the same way, at the same rate, or have the same mental or physical capabilities. They ARE all the same in the sense that all are a wonderful gift to parent, teacher, society. They all have a success potential to help themselves, their family and mankind. The teacher's job is to help children reach their maximum success potential, but their differences will dictate which direction the teacher will take for each child.

So, who is that child that strolls into your classroom, all happy, at least for the first day? And what difference does a difference make, anyway? For a teacher, all the difference in the world. In the world of automobiles, cars are all considered cars, but a Ferrari is not built the same as a Pinto and performs differently. Don't get me wrong, they will both get you to the grocery store, but I don't recall that many trophy winners having their picture taken next to their forest green Pinto. You could even give it a snazzy paint job with flames running down the side so it even resembles the Ferrari, but I suggest that is a little much for trips to the grocery store. So, how is your child built, internally, mentally, physically?

Many children who come into the classroom may have had a heavy dose of *positive childhood experiences*. They are healthy and they have had a proper diet with which to build brain function. They have been exposed to a large and positive vocabulary from parents; reading in the household is a normal and enjoyable event, for parent and child. They have had exposure to interesting places and a variety of people. Television and other media is limited and monitored. They have parents who have time to spend with their child and actually do, in positive ways. At least one of the parents works at a decent job and there is enough money in the family so that the child has an inner sense of security. They are loved and wanted and seen as a positive element in the family. Speaking of a feeling of security, they may come from a home with two parents, both the original set.

Then there are the children that come to the classroom with a trailer truck load of *negative childhood experiences*. There is virtually no money in the household and the family is under constant financial stress; because of the financial stress the child may be seen as a burden, not a well spring of joy. The child may have not even been wanted in the first place, retarding the love bonding between parent and child. Parents may be divorced. They may be overworked. Some may be single parents, stuck in a job that doesn't pay well, leaving the parent exhausted and with very little time to actually raise their child. There could be violence in the household or community. Some children are exposed to a limited and often negative vocabulary from the adults in their life, including nonstop cursing. Alcohol or drug abuse can serve to mask the grim reality of the adult's life. Crime can sometimes fill the void for zero job opportunities in economically depressed areas. Children may have relatives or friends in prison, which they may look up to as their role models, since they ARE relatives or friends. Poor nutrition or prenatal care may limit child brain development. Television may be on 24/7, much of it unsupervised or poorly supervised while there is virtually no reading or intellectually stimulating activities in the house. Some children have very little exposure to a variety of places or people; etc., etc., etc.

The experiences that a child brings to the classroom are going to dictate, to a certain extent, how teachers will run their classroom. Studies have shown over and over that experiences that shape children's brain development and ability to learn from birth to three years old are, in a very real sense, one half of the ballgame in regards to how successful they will be in school and later on in their adult life. Take a deep breath and let that sink in for a minute. As a teacher, if you in your heart of hearts want all of your children to succeed in life, you have got to know that child intimately and what skill set they bring to you in your class. Children that come from poverty and economically depressed households carry more baggage with them than Aunt Ruth going on a two month vacation. It is all internal, so Jimmy, the wealthy child from Sunnybrook Farm and Jack, the poor child from Failure, USA, look the same, but are in fact very different children. The effects of poverty and negative life experiences have profound and sometimes lasting effects on children. So does wealth and positive life experiences. So, get to know your children really, really well. And enjoy it. Children are cool to be around no matter what their background, especially if you don't let the Byzantine rules and regulations of a school system sour you on the experience.

Forces at Play on the Teacher

There was a time, deep in the murky recesses of the past, that teachers actually ran the classroom and were in total charge of their domain. I was in an antique store in Michigan once, and came across a painting of a teacher in a log cabin type of one room schoolhouse. In front of her was a group of children of all ages, humped over at their desks, working feverishly. The teacher was a slight but stern middle aged woman, pointing at a student with the long switch in her hand, evidently asking a child to read, and meaning it. It was a picture of complete and total classroom control by a supremely confident woman going about her duties as teacher, one of the single most important people in the entire community. It was only thirty dollars, but being a modern day teacher, I couldn't afford it, and left it hanging there on the wall. I still have the image of that woman in my head, (Did I mention stern?) and crack up every time I think about it. If that picture were to be painted today it would be of a young woman (teachers on average are only lasting about five years now) weeping in the corner because she can't understand the 32nd adjustment to the new, Soviet-style five year plan that somebody, somewhere has hatched up, the $4.50 that she has been given for supplies is used up, the copy machine is broken and Suzie's parents are on the way to beat her up because Suzy got a "B" instead of an "A". Welcome to the brave new world of classroom micromanagement and handwringing. It would all be funny if it wasn't. And it all impacts directly on the teacher's ability to teach.

What is really weird is that some people back in the mid-1800's, around the time of the aforementioned one room schoolhouse, saw this coming. Three of America's leading writers, Ralph Waldo Emerson, Walt Whitman and Henry David Thoreau, were proponents of a train of thought called Transcendental Individualism. They believed that the power of America to be great depended on the power of an individual to be great. They were afraid that the powers of government bureaucracies and corporate power were going to drown the individual's power to do great things. Their books could have been written an hour ago. Their books would also be one hundred and fifty years too late, but I'd recommend buying one anyway. It is hard to be a great teacher when you are being told what to do all the time. It is even harder when what you are being told to do isn't necessarily right. It might be right, sort of, but may not be right for that individual child sitting in front of you that may need something different. Then you go into the "Should I actually teach this child and maybe she'll stop crying or should I keep my job so I can eat?" internal debate. Eating usually wins. I was scolded once for making reading fun by making the kids laugh during a hypnotically boring *scripted* reading lesson. Laughter wasn't in the script and deviation is a cardinal sin. Don't get me started! Sometimes teachers will find themselves at the end of the day when things didn't go so well, according to script, as it were, wondering "What is the matter here? I've got all of these behavior problems and if the learning gains don't improve, I've gone through four years of college to work at a fast food restaurant. What is the matter with me?" Well, possibly nothing. This is a VERY comforting thought, one which allowed me to keep my sanity in the classroom. It could very well be the spider web of bureaucracy that you are enmeshed in, since you actually have little to say over how, or what, or at what rate you teach little Jimmy. The teacher simply can't tell if they are any good, and can't even dream of aspiring to greatness, if they are not allowed to follow their instincts and are being bossed around all day long. *The reason why I am belaboring this point is that all children, especially those that are struggling academically and behaviorally, and those coming from negative backgrounds such as poverty and violence, need really good teachers to save their lives.* There is a reason that the national average burnout rate for teachers is five years, and it isn't just the lousy pay. This begs the question: "How do I become a GOOD TEACHER if I have so little control over my day?" To start with, simply ignore the man behind the curtain. At least until you finish reading all of this. Then, and only then, will we factor in what the powers that be want. In the meantime, I will build, step by step, what it means to teach children, regardless of their background, to their optimum success levels and to give them the academic and emotional skills necessary to not just survive, but flourish as an adult. To help them reach their divine purpose for being here on this planet, to reach their destiny. THAT is teaching. I figured some things out over the last several decades because for me, for years, there was no man behind the curtain. I taught Exceptional Education in a portable out back of a dysfunctional high school in an economically depressed setting. There was only one rule, "If your kids don't show up at the principal's office, you're doing a great job." What at the time seemed total abandonment with a side order of lack of support turned out to be a blessing in disguise. I learned how to teach. For real. How to save children's lives under excruciating stress. Let me share a few things that I have learned so that maybe you will have an easier time of it, have a lasting and positive impact on the children that you are privileged to come in contact with, find enjoyment from the exhilaration of successful teaching, and hopefully stay in the classroom a lot longer than five years. God bless teachers everywhere.

Before we go on to SETTING the STAGE, let me add two quick points. In places where teachers have little control over their actual teaching, or are in high stakes, test-driven systems the teachers will feel a buildup of stress. Unnecessary, inappropriate, but very real stress. *Teachers, be aware of it and absolutely do not pass that stress on to the children!* You have to be their shield from all of this nonsense. This is doubly important for the bottom 25% of your children, those who don't do so well in school, because they don't have the internal strength that successful children have and may buckle like a cardboard box in a thunderstorm. If you find yourself holding a bullhorn up to a child's ear and shrieking, "Come on, I know you can read faster than that! What's the matter with you? And stop that whimpering, it's upsetting Kevin!" it is a hint that you are under just a tad too much pressure. That's when you take a deep breath and repeat, "It's not the child, it's the man behind the curtain" ten times. After you center yourself, put down the bullhorn, pick the child up, dust him off, and go on with reading pleasantly. The other quick point is, as a teacher, you don't like the forty-six cruel but creative ways the powers that be come up with every year in their quest to punish you into being a successful teacher, think of this punishment—leads—to-success mentality from the child's point of view. Now, there's an eye-opener.

Part Two:
Setting the Stage for Success

Teacher's Self-View

"How much power do you think a teacher has these days?" This is a question I often hear teachers ask when they are at their wits end, eyes tearing up, their disrespect cup full to the brim. Being disrespected by children and not feeling like you can control the situation is about as unpleasant as it gets for a teacher, especially a new one. They are often under the impression that all children are going to like them because they are, after all, a teacher, for heaven's sake. I often get a variation of the word "none." I will nod my head in sympathy, and then say, "Watch this." On one particular occasion I had come to see what I could do for a temporary teacher who was holding down an exceptional education class next to mine after I had received her SOS signal. I walked into the classroom, mentally picked out the unruliest child, and asked that young lady to please sit down. After getting a very colorful response that I took to mean "no", I calmly picked up the phone, called the office and informed them to get Linda's paperwork in order, because she was going to be transferred to another school, where possibly this kind of behavior would be accepted. She was still yelling, "You can't do that!" as the security guard dragged her down to the office. She wasn't too big on the reality thing, evidently. The rest of the class had a much better grasp on the concept of reality, and fairly quickly were paying rapt attention to my utterly fascinating lecture on how you can be anything you wish to be in life, if you have the desire and the SELF CONTROL to get there. Well, they may not have been fascinated so much as quiet, but you take what you can get. I leaned over to the teacher and said, *"Teachers have all the power they want."*

I came to this realization out of desperation years ago when it dawned upon me that no outside help was coming to deal with my student problems in any real sense, so either man-up or go home. And the students, contrary to their behavior, badly needed me in their lives. Instead of looking outside for strength, I looked inside, which is exactly where I found it. I should probably apologize to Rosa Parks, and to my readers, because I constantly use her as an example in everything I write, but she is the embodiment of power through a strong view of self. One day she was an underpaid, overworked maid, which is probably the one profession that is more powerless than a teacher. The next day she became the very symbol of the civil rights movement because her view of her self-worth as a human being had changed.

Your power as a teacher will come from your view of what it means to be a teacher. If being a teacher to you is just a job, and not a very good one at that, you are indeed powerless. When the disrespect comes, you will be out looking for a real job that actually pays something. If, on the other hand, you view teaching as a calling and something akin to spiritual you may begin to view teaching as the single most important profession on the planet because all other professions flow from it. You may come to believe that children will be lost in our society without the skills that you provide in your classroom and that our very system of democracy is dependent on an educated citizenry. You may see that for many families the only way out of poverty is for their children to not only become educated, but socialized in positive behaviors that will lead toward success in life. As a teacher, you may come to realize that you are not just a role model but may very well be the only truly functioning adult in a child's life. Without you, there is a very real possibility that a struggling child might become lost not only to themselves but also their latent talents to society as well. Now THAT is a self-view that is not only worth getting out of bed for, but will carry you through the most trying of times, which are the times that children need you the most. It is this self-view of teacher that allows a good one to just cut a glance at a misbehaving child and they straighten up. The child's behavioral change doesn't come from the look, but from what is behind the look. A person that believes he is important and powerful IS important and powerful. This point of view will help you deal effectively with unruly adults, also. The ones who think phrases like, "If you can't do, teach" are actually funny and repeat them endlessly at parties. Once you have gotten your mind right and realize how important you really are, you are now ready to enter a classroom and do some real good.

Child's Self View

What children think of themselves is, in many ways, the single most important thing that they bring with them to the classroom. Children with a positive view of themselves, that they are basically "good", are WAY different children to teach than ones who view themselves as "bad." The children that have a self concept that that they are "good" probably had a fairly positive upbringing which transfers to a positive view of life in general. They view what the future has for them in a positive light. They often know what they want to do when they grow up. They have positive life goals. Children that have the negative self concept of being "bad" often have had an upbringing filled with a lot of negative experiences, which can lead to a negative view of life in general. They may view what the future has for them in a negative light. They often don't have a clue as to what they want to do later in life and are goal-less, which has a direct impact on their thinking. It leans more towards the "What can I do to make myself happy right now?" kind than "I will try hard to improve myself" kind, and for some odd reason always find themselves in trouble. Being in trouble a lot impacts everybody else's thinking and negative things become expected of the "bad" child. If they struggle academically long enough, they begin to view their label of "being bad" with pride, because that has become their power source, because their REAL power source, their intellect, isn't generating any power. The only thing their intellect is generating is a steady stream of humiliating experiences, which, if they weren't bad before, will drive them that way. The only way to deal with a child with a "bad" self-view is to structure your class experiences so that they experience a lot of success academically and behaviorally and are rewarded for it. Over time you can actually create a child who thinks deep down inside that he is "good." You will, in fact, have saved that child's life. This is where the teacher's self-view needs to be King-Kong size, encompassing much more than just teaching Algebra. *Children from negative backgrounds have got to have their school day systematically set up to receive a lot of positive, successful experiences.* More on this later, once we enter the class.

Why do some children act one way and some act another? Why does one child reach over and help Carlita pick up her crayons when she drops them, when a second child would just laugh at her, a third might thump her on her head as she leans over, and a fourth might simply use the chaos as a perfect time to steal crayons? Well, normal is normal. Children will react to situations as to what they perceive is normal, to them. How they were raised and their life circumstances will dictate what is normal to them. Two polar examples will suffice. I was talking with a friend a while back about the Manning family. Archie Manning, the dad and one of the all-time great quarterbacks, had two sons who also went on to become all-time great quarterbacks: Peyton Manning and Eli Manning. My friend's remark was along the lines of what a great gene pool in that family. That the young Mannings had inherited great football genes, if there is such a thing. I am not a believer in football genes. I said, "No, I don't think so. I think that while growing up in that household, they viewed being a great quarterback as NORMAL. Same as sons or daughters of great musicians or singers growing up to be great musicians and singers themselves. They grew up surrounded by parents and their friends of greatness and it was their normal life. To drop it back a peg, if a child is raised in a family where the parents and other relatives and neighbors have gone to college, it is just normal in their mind that they will, too. It doesn't mean that they are going to, but the idea of it isn't a stretch at all. If you are an astronaut's son or daughter, the thought of you growing up to be an astronaut isn't farfetched because they have actually seen it done, whereas, if my dad had turned to me and said that I would grow up to be an astronaut, I would have told him to back away from his Martini glass.

To go to the opposite end of the success world, let's visit failure land for a while. I read a statistic somewhere that said that if a parent or relative of a child has been in prison there is a 75% chance of that child getting caught up in the criminal justice system, also. My mind seized up with a loud, "Whoa, hoss. Slow that down so that I can think about THAT for a while." And thought about it I did. I have seen what happens when children grow up where doing bad things is simply normal. I was a discipline coordinator for a county for a year. Thursday is juvenile court day and I would sit with a child's school records on my lap, which would sometimes help a child if they were actually trying to succeed in school, or they would sink a child if it became clear that he only went to school to eat. I have watched the parade of orange jumpsuits long enough to know that most of the children in front of me were not bad children, but had grown up believing that whatever type of behavior had put them in jail was normal because it was WAY too normal where they grew up. Children will act and behave in ways that reflect how they were raised, and cannot do otherwise. It is not a child's fault that she was surrounded by stupidity, anger, violence, and outrageous conduct when she was an infant. Do not hold it against the child. Do something about it! They don't have to grow up to be the 75%. They can be the 25% that make it, if you, the teacher, decide that child will succeed, at whatever cost, including your own skyrocketing blood pressure. It can be done if you have a gigantic self-view as teacher and understand the forces at play on your children.

Teacher's View of the Child

All children were put on this planet for a positive purpose as an adult. All children, from anywhere, that look like anything, regardless of their background can be positive, successful adults. If one of these two statements isn't in your belief system, do yourself and your students a favor and become a carpenter, air plane pilot, or something that has nothing to do with raising children. If you came out of college thinking that you were just going to teach subject matter and were going to leave the child raising thing to overworked, underpaid, stressed out parents, become a lawyer, go back to said school, and sue them.

Your faith in the inherent worth of each child is the fuel that drives everything that you do in the classroom. Very few people that aren't teachers actually know this, but teaching, if done properly, is the most mentally, emotionally and in some sense physically demanding job in the world. That is why at the end of the day they find themselves drained and by Friday are talking about some version of Happy Hour. And this is teaching the "good" students. To teach a lot of students that are struggling either academically or behaviorally you have got to have a rock solid belief in their positive future, and that your Herculean efforts to get them there is worthwhile in the long run, or else you will burn out. I have been teaching for a LONG time, which allows me the pleasure to occasionally see the results of my efforts. When I receive a "Hi, Mr. Hoatson, remember me?" from a young man wearing a suit and holding his beautiful child in his arms, when the only suit that he was headed for when he was younger was one with stripes and a number on it, it is more than gratifying, it is life confirming. The problem is that most teachers don't last a long time anymore and never get to see the results of their efforts in any real way. Unyielding faith in your children will help you not be so tired at the end of the week, because you will have a sense of satisfaction. You will internally reward yourself for your efforts, even if seemingly nobody else does.

It helps to cultivate a belief system by looking at historical examples of people who have come from ridiculously harsh and negative backgrounds but went on to become somebody successful. My favorite real life story is Ray Charles, because he grew up as a child an hour and a half drive from my house. I used to take my daughter to the little park where his bronze statue is and let her play there, while I would stare at the statue in wonderment. How in the world an impoverished blind child could grow up to be a world renowned piano player, singer and songwriter, is beyond me. Just the piano playing part is beyond me. But it happened, which is the point. *Anything is possible*. That child that just kicked Annabelle, your model student, out of frustration and spite, could be the same child that becomes an EMT that saves Annabelle's life by navigating his ambulance through traffic to get her to the hospital in the nick of time. This anything is possible belief will help carry you through any and all rough spots in your school experience, allowing you to not only be an effective teacher, but to become a long-lasting experienced effective teacher. You will actually be there in the classroom when the children need you instead of daily scouring the want ads for what the private sector world would call a "real job."

Part Three:
In the Classroom, In the Beginning

The Parent is Your Best Friend

Now, the average parent is not necessarily going to start out being your best friend. Some parents hated school when they were children and it seems that time hasn't put a pleasant glow on their experiences. Some parents have children that are not all that well behaved, have received numerous phone calls from the school through the years pointing this fact out to them, and have learned to pretend that they have no phone, with a straight face, yet. Other parents have children that are very slow learners, whose children are bordering on a nervous breakdown daily because they can't keep up with the pace set for them by bureaucrats who seem to drink way too much coffee, and are sick of their children crying themselves to sleep at night. Some parents have five jobs and work 32 hours a day and have trouble remembering who their child actually is or what he looks like. Or was it a she? And then there is the parent who loved school, has a bright and happy child, and looks forward to volunteering and lending a helping hand whenever she can. Call her last.

When you first enter your classroom at the first second of the first day, look for the phone and get ready to use it. After you have actually met their child call mom or dad and tell them what a wonderful child they have, that she is going to have a great year and that you are blessed to have the privilege to teach a wonderful child such as this. Use the word wonderful a lot, even if their behavior has already caught the attention of the security guard. *Positive parent contact at the beginning of the year is probably the single most important action that you can take as a teacher to ensure that your children succeed in your class.* It seems like a pleasant but simple task, but the power of the positive phone call is layered with ramifications that will play out in your classroom all year long. The first thing it does is set up in the parent's mind that you are on their child's side, that you have the best interest of their child in the foremost part of *your* mind, and that you want that child to succeed, not fail. In short, it sends the message is that you like their child. Trust me on this one. If a parents know that you like their child, and the child feels welcomed and liked by the teacher, the task of actually educating or disciplining that child has just become ten times easier than if you had never made that phone call. This is especially true if that positive phone call is to parents who distrust the school or teachers in general and have had negative experiences with schools either themselves, or through their child, or often both. Homes that are mired in financial problems and are stressed by other factors such as divorce, substance abuse, anger, etc., are already filled with negativity and they simply can't take on any more. If the first phone call that a teacher makes to a struggling household is negative in nature, their child has done this or that bad thing, the schoolhouse will automatically be shut off from the house. This is the very last thing that a teacher wants, because a good education for that child might be the only thing that saves that family. The children who misbehave are the ones that need a good classroom experience the most, because their misbehaviors are sometimes a pretty good indication that their home life isn't going so well. If there is a positive bond between the teacher and a struggling family whose child is also struggling at school, then there is a lifeline thrown from the school to the parent that the parent just might grab onto. *The positive bond between teacher and parent allows for positive advice tips on how to help the child academically or behaviorally, or positive parenting tips on what to do at the home to help the child, to actually be heeded because the teacher is viewed as a friend to the family.* This heeded thing is important, because you can give all the great advice you want to, but if you are viewed as hostile to a child or a parent, you might as well "talk to the hand." It is important to keep in mind that, in my experience, almost all academic or behavioral problems originated in the home and you can't fix a lot of the child's problems in isolation from the classroom. The better the child succeeds in the house the better the child will succeed in the class, and it goes the other way, also. If the child is disrespecting the teacher, secretary and his entire class, chances are he is not the model of politeness at home. The more that a classroom is set up for success experiences for a struggling child, and those success experiences can be duplicated at the house, the sooner the idea of success is internalized in that child so that it becomes second nature, or "normal." The teacher and parent will be thanking each other profusely by the end of the year. *The parents of children who behave the worst or whose children are woefully behind academically need you the most. Be there for them.* At first blush, the parent phone call will be seen by teachers as just one more chore to do and the suggestion to make the calls will be met with grunting, groaning, or other angry animal type noises; maybe even hissing if it comes at the end of a too long faculty meeting. From my experience, not only are positive phone calls to parents not a chore, they are the most fun that a teacher can ever have. The more you make, the more you want to make. My suggestion is, pour it on. "Mr. Gonzalez, guess what, Pedro just wrote a perfect paragraph. I'm not kidding. He just read it to the principal, and I'm hanging it on the wall here. When he writes his first book I want it autographed. And free, being his teacher and all. Sure, you can say hi. Here he is." That conversation took exactly 15 seconds. When Pedro first got to class he couldn't spell the word "cat" much less write a paragraph. Think about what is going through Dad's head right now. And Pedro's. That 15 seconds of your time could be the most positive thing that has happened in that family for the entire week. And wait until they tell Grandma! And let me tell you something, as a teacher when I was having a bad day at the factory, I would reach for that phone and make that call and my entire day would change instantly, because if nothing else I had just done some real good for a child. And even better, once you've had about ten of these quick and positive conversations with a parent the eleventh one can be that Pedro seemed a little cranky today as evidenced by him throwing books at his classmates heads, and that maybe he should get to bed a little earlier because 1:00 a.m. seems to be pushing it, *and that conversation will be pleasant, also.* If a positive bond hadn't been built up before the negative phone call to Pedro's Dad, it may have ended way differently, with Dad making his own phone call to the principal telling her that he is tired of teachers picking on his kid. Pedro is not the only one who can be cranky, especially since Dad gets zero sleep because of his two jobs. The lesson to all of this is that not only is the positive phone call not a chore, but will, over time, make your whole teaching day not a chore. Now THAT is worth 15 seconds every once in a while.

One last word, or phrase actually, on effective communication with parents: judge not, lest ye be judged. Being nonjudgmental of parents is vitally important if you are going to help educate the child being raised in a truly dysfunctional family. I had a child that I had to drive home every once in a while, his behavior being such on some days that I knew he wouldn't make it thirty feet down the road on the bus. I would call Mrs. White in advance and she would meet me in front of her run down trailer, dressed in an old bathrobe, ratty bedroom slippers, hair in curlers, beer in left hand, cigarette in right hand, eyeballing little Johnny suspiciously, and ask how he did that day, and what she could do to help. I didn't actually have a crazy person in front of me, I had a caring parent. That is all the information that I need to help that family. And since I never pointed out certain things, such as her dressing habits at 4:00 PM, her joblessness, her brand of beer was cheap and the cigarettes were going to kill everybody within 20 feet of her and she needed to something, anything with that hair, she didn't view me as a threat and in fact tried very hard to listen and do as I suggested. She knew the only two things that she needed to know, that I liked her son and that I had his best interests in mind. She would read to him at night because I explained that it would build a certain portion of his brain and she would go get him puzzles from who knows where because that builds the math part of his brain, and she would eventually do her cigarette smoking outside with her sisters so that the atmosphere in the house would stay clean for the boy. The brand of beer would stay the same. There's no telling for taste. I have found that ALL parents in dire circumstances, whether they are unemployed, have criminal records, are battling addictions or are illiterate, abused, alone or whatever, ALL parents want better for their child. Many simply are deeply lost trying to find success in their own lives, and are equally lost in trying to find success for their children. If you don't judge a "bad" parent, they will not run from you, because nobody actually actively strives to be a bad parent. The teacher and schoolhouse need to be a safe harbor for the child AND parent so that the family can get positive, constructive help. Many of the academic and behavioral problems at the school will come from dysfunctional parents. You need to be welcomed into their lives with a smile, reflecting the smile on your face. You don't necessarily have to accept the beer being offered. These are the families that need clear and positive communication between the school house and the home the most. Give them LOTS of good phone calls whenever their Johnny is performing well at school. Purposely catch him doing well and call. Society will thank you for it. And it's fun.

Creating a Classroom Atmosphere: Part 1

Loving and Kind

If a child feels loved by the teacher 90% of the teacher's behavioral problems tend to evaporate or at least become very manageable. The child will also be in the frame of mind to do his best work, to keep that loving feeling going. I have done what seems a lifetime of cafeteria duty and found that the best way to keep law and order is to be proactive. I would greet every child by name, laugh and joke with them, hug them (age appropriate—elementary school) or slap hands or bump fists, and horse around a lot. It creates a "Life is really good" atmosphere, which is important in the morning before you send children off to class. I could gage who was in a good mood or not, and then pull aside the "or nots" and figure out why not, do a little mood repair, and send them on their way smiling. This was in a cafeteria on a mass scale.

For the classroom it becomes much easier because of the fewer numbers and the amount of time spent with the children. They are literally YOUR children. So, set the tone of the day from the get-go. Stand at the door and greet each child with a bombardment of goodwill:

Jimmy my man, looking sharp today. Cornelius, let me feel that head of yours. Yep, you got the smart head today, I feel genius up in there. What in the world do I feel around my waist? It must be some kind of a wild creature. No, it's not, it's Brianna. Can you have a hug? What do I look like to you, the hug man? I do, huh, well then come get two. Rosalita, how's my doctor doing today? Remember, when you get rich I get 20%. Shanterica, come here my grumpy girl. It's impossible to be in a bad mood today—the birds are singing, we've been blessed with food, so what's up? Michelle stole your pencil? You mean that little yellow nub you've been dragging around here. Well, we'll show Michelle a thing or two. Go to my desk and get a brand new special metallic blue one. Make it three of them so you can treat your friends. Lavonte, what did your dad say last night after I bragged on you? You went out to dinner? And you didn't take me? Don't get cheap on me, boy. Wait just a doggone minute, are my eyes deceiving me or is everybody at their desk on time today? You've got to be kidding me. Well, as they say in <u>Lawrence of Arabia,</u> "I am a fountain for my people." Metallic blue pencils for everybody!

Now, if the children had enough paper-mache' they would build a life size statue to you and put it in the middle of the room after the start to the day like that. Do it daily. It's easy and fun and the children will run home and tell mom what a great time they had in school, making parent contact easy and fun. Heaven forbid that the school experience is fun, for student, teacher and parent. You can create a loving atmosphere at any grade level at any time. There are several practical reasons to do so.

The first is behavioral management. If a child likes you and you like them, they will do their best to please you and will take whatever discipline measures that you occasionally need without freaking out, because you have a good, positive relationship with that child. I have found that laughter is the best bonding glue of all. If the teacher and the child have shared a few good laughs together it opens the gateway into each other's hearts, putting a positive sheen on all further interactions, including discipline. Especially including discipline. If you are a teacher and haven't laughed in the last six months, take a vacation, watch a lot of Cosby, Sinbad or Steve Martin and then come back into the classroom. Your children will love you for it. The second reason is that the teaching of academics becomes much easier, especially for the struggling child, because it takes the fear, frustration and anger emotions out of the picture, which are paralyzing to struggling students. This cannot be stressed enough and I will stress it more specifically later, but the last thing that a child who is behind academically and exhibits trouble with reading needs is to be constantly afraid of the teacher's reactions to their lousy academic performance. The teacher doesn't want the struggling child to have to check over their shoulder every thirty seconds to see if the teacher is smiling or getting ready to scold them. The smile should always be there, even if the child proudly came up with 3 plus 3=105. If the academic experience is always pleasant then the teacher will always get the best effort from each child, which will facilitate the optimum learning for each child. It is not the child's fault that the "man behind the curtain" thinks that this child should be doing better. If the children are happy and not quaking with fear each time they approach a sheet of paper, chances are that not only will they learn the material but may actually run to school instead of watching "The Great Escape" over and over to get this tunneling thing down right. The third reason is a little deep, but very important. If you greet a child lovingly, every single day, no matter WHAT he had done the day before, it allows the chronically misbehaving child to be "born again" in a behavioral sense every day, giving him a chance, over time, to shift to better behaviors. The teacher's steadfast love for that child is gigantic for the misbehaving child to change his behavior. The fact that little Brandon, who called you fat stupid and bald the day before can be met with a "My man Brandon, how's my junior fireman doing today?" instead of, "Good Lord, it's you again. What are you doing here?" could mean the difference in the long run between his actually becoming a fireman or dropping out of school and becoming Brandon the thug. Now, the name calling of the teacher will be dealt with, in no uncertain terms, THAT DAY. Probably that minute. But then it's done. Tomorrow is a new day for that child and that teacher and that steadfast love and loving atmosphere will ensure that tomorrow is indeed a new and positive day.

Purposely cultivating amnesia is a good trait for teachers to practice. This becomes easier if the teacher never takes anything personally, even if it was meant that way, or seemed that way at the time. If a child is so out of control that they are flagrantly disrespecting you, remember, IT IS PROBABLY NOT YOU that they are disrespecting. They are releasing anger your way, but if you were replaced by someone else the anger would still be released in the same direction. Children who are out of control often have large problems with any authority figures, because that person is trying to control them, and they are simply not used to it, because they are lacking a controlling figure in their lives and have not developed any respect for proper authority, whether parent, teacher, police officer, etc. Stay within your all-important, Rock of Gibraltar self-view as Teacher with a capital "T" and let bounce off of you any even slight indication of hurt feelings, with a calm and cool, "Have you lost your mind, this is a school, here" attitude. The more omniscient and in control you act, the more you actually are, preserving the loving atmosphere in the class, even in the face of misbehaviors. I have seen positive relationships and wonderful atmosphere in a classroom turn sour over a period of time because of a teacher yelling at students. If it happens often enough the atmosphere in the class becomes corrosive, even when things are going well for a while. One of the secrets that I have discovered, and have taken to heart, is that if you yell at one child, you are yelling at them all, even the good kids. It fills the room with poison which lingers and which no air freshener can really cover. It also is a sign that the teacher is out of control of a situation, otherwise he wouldn't be yelling. (Memo to the powers that be: it is hard for your teachers to maintain a positive, loving, efficient learning atmosphere for the children when the teacher is in a constant state of irritation because of near constant bureaucratic meddling. How about spending your busy day trying to figure out what to do *for* teachers, not *to* teachers?) Anyway, stay in control with a hugely inflated view of the importance of being a teacher, a sunny disposition, really thick, rhino type of skin, and a healthy dose of amnesia. It is vitally important that you keep a loving and friendly atmosphere for the children, because it will bring about their best, both as students and as human beings. True story: I was on the way to give a lecture on the power of nonviolence to a group of teenagers who were in trouble with the school system because of fighting. Their parents and siblings were also in attendance. As I was entering the room I passed a little boy, probably around eight years old, and judging by his body language was in a foul mood. "What's up my man?" I said as I was passing him. "Shut up, you old cracker," was his response. This is where "The problem obviously doesn't reside in me" teacher automatic response needs to kick in so that you don't say something stupid to a troubled child, allowing you later to help said troubled child. And it did, because I have cultivated it. "Well aren't we the grumpy Gus?" I responded in an amused tone, walked inside and gave a really good lecture. When I was done I was shaking hands with students and their families, but I was having a little trouble, because I had a small child who evidently loved my lecture, clinging to my leg the whole time I was glad handing everybody else. Old grumpy Gus, I found out later, had his candy taken away from him by his Grandmother and put out of the room to chill out. I was the first person he saw, and not only was he not chilled, he was red hot. So, there you go. *Lesson one*: a positive or at least neutral response to a bad situation will always leave the door open for the misbehaving child to change his behavior to a more positive one later, because they have not been attacked and thus, have nothing to defend. *Lesson two*: A loving atmosphere is not in the room, it is in you the teacher, and will permeate whatever room you are in. What underpins all of this is the knowledge that your children in your classroom know that you love them unconditionally, no matter what crazy thing they may have just done. *Unconditional love for children is the creator and keeper of the positive atmosphere in any classroom.*

The last thing I will say about creating a loving atmosphere in the classroom is probably the most important. Some children come from homes or communities that are undergoing serious hardships and the home experience for some children is less than loving and kind. Sometimes it is awash in negativity, meaning that a loving and kind classroom may be their only real hope for a positive adulthood. It is not an accident that many children that struggle academically or behaviorally have real struggles at the house. To get them to succeed in life they need to be fertilized with love and care someplace, and that place just might be your classroom. Pour on the love. Not only is it effective on so many levels, but is free to the school system. You can't beat that.

On a personal note: I used to have a fairly sloppy classroom, appearance-wise. Neatness was not one of my top priorities and I have zero artistic sense. You could tell that immediately by looking at my bulletin board. One day I was actually paying attention at a faculty meeting and the principal was trying to make the point that many of the children come from pretty shabby houses and the least the faculty could do was make their classrooms look decent. He wasn't often right, but he was dead on target that day. I changed my sorry ways. A nice atmosphere in the class extends to its physical appearance, big time. Disneyland it up. Or career land it up. Or art land it up. The teacher and the child are going to spend a third of their life in that class and the physical appearance can be manipulated to create a wonderful visual atmosphere. Children coming from sterile or negative home environments can use all the doses of positivity that they can get. Eye-popping and thought provoking physical surroundings are a great visual backdrop for the eye-popping and thought provoking learning that takes place inside those classroom walls.

Creating a Classroom Atmosphere: Part Two

Whatever Else You Do, Don't Be Boring!!!

There are three exclamation points up there for a reason. Studies, classroom experience and just plain old common sense will tell you a very important pedagogical concept: All real learning is emotion based. If something is interesting to the student the material will not only be absorbed, but also retained. Boring stuff may or may not be absorbed, at least temporarily, but the chances of retention approach zero. Raise your hand if you can tell the difference between a Doric and Corinthian Column. If you can, you were probably interested in Greek architecture and found this type of subject matter fascinating. When I was submersed in the same subject, I was either staring longingly at Suzie across the classroom, or adjusting the noose around my neck because the boredom was reaching jump off the stool proportions. I can't really remember because I didn't retain anything that day. Rule of thumb: If the teacher's mind goes numb just staring at the textbook and the snoring sounds are audible clear at the back of the class, this is not a good sign for the students. If you are bored, your students will be double bored, but unlike you, will find outrageous ways to entertain themselves. Not necessarily funny, but entertaining nonetheless. This rule of thumb takes on greater importance in the light of the fact that some of the modern day textbooks are so watered down and dumbed down that the Battle of Gettysburg, which, if told properly, should have the hair on your head standing straight up, which won't be noticed because you are wiping the tears from your eyes, is now described in three sentences which read like "Blah, blah, blah and then Lincoln showed up and said something." This type of lesson is not only the kiss of death in a behavioral management sense, but in a material retention sense as well. When the African American children in class, after studying the Civil War for two weeks come up during a review for the test and ask, "Now, who were the slaveholders, again? Were they wearing Blue or Gray? I want to make sure I get a good grade on my test," this is a clear signal that something has gone somewhat awry in the classroom.

Making it interesting can have benefits for the teacher as well as the students, because interesting can often be translated into fun. I was in a vocabulary expanding mood one day surrounded by my Headstart three year olds and wanted to teach the concept of propulsion. My lecture consisted of blowing up a balloon and letting fly around the room, swooping over their heads while they screamed in delight. Those children learned more about science in one day than your average seventh grader learns in a month. The excitement made the vocabulary stick like glue. During a middle school class which was all snoozing over the concept of metrics, I caught a girl sneaking some sort of pork rind chips out of a bag. I took the bag and read the label. "Very curious, I didn't even know that this much fat was possible in a bag so small. Hold out your hand, sweetheart, I'm going to put 35 grams in it." I went and got thirty five gram weights and placed them in her hand and then yelled to a kid in the back of the class, GET THE HEART PUMP JIMMY, SHE'S GOING TO BLOW!" Amidst the gales of laughter, they forever learned what a gram was. In a science class once I casually mentioned the old, "There are more stars in the universe than all the grains of sand in all of the beaches on Earth" chestnut, which seemed to get the students heads spinning a bit. When a bright young lady chirped up with the question, "How big is the universe, anyway?" I casually responded with, "They don't really know, it's still expanding," which elicited the "WHAT@#^*?" response that every teacher craves, because it shows actual thinking going on inside of a child's head. Un-boring a child may be the best favor that you can for them, because it may set off a train of events in that child's head that may even approach a love for learning. The un-boring of a child becomes vital when that child is actively hostile to anything that smacks of school and thinks that using his real power source of being able to terrorize the neighborhood is actually going to be a fruitful career move. "Bump you, man. You can't make me read!!" Let me add the fact that the student is not usually smiling when he blurts out something of this nature in the teacher's direction. There is, in fact, no student in any real sense inside that tensed up body that is glowering at the teacher, meaning somebody that is interested in learning something that the teacher has to offer. It is now time to create a student through interest. "Why in the world would I want to teach you to read? I'm not about to jeopardize my life. I've got a family to think about." "What in the world are you talking about?" "What I am talking about is that if this was 1840 and I was in a state where it was illegal, as in government law type of illegal, to teach any and all African American children to read, and the sheriff found about it I would be dragged out of my house in the middle of the night and hung by my neck in the town square. This is so that everybody that gazed upon my corpse would learn a really big lesson, which is that if you teach a slave to read it is an act of revolution. They might become powerful and not only refuse to be slaves but might educate other slaves not to be slaves which may then lead to something like a civil war with soldiers of color pouring into the south to free their enslaved families, which was a bigoted southerners worst nightmare. Anyway, that was the theory—that brain power was 100 times more powerful than physical power, and slaves are, by definition, powerless. I shouldn't have to be telling you any of this boring stuff because if you READ YOUR BOOK you would know this." The last time I saw that young man he had barricaded himself in the library and the principal was trying to talk him out, using a bullhorn. That young man had become a student . . . a good one.

Make your lessons interesting. That's all a teacher has to do, ever, for learning to take place. Interesting lessons have the added benefit of making knowledge retention last a long time, instead of just three days until the test. Engaging lessons have the double added benefit of dropping behavioral problems to almost none, making the teacher's job much easier and giving them more time and energy to create interesting lessons. It also does wonders for whatever disciplinarians are working at the school. It frees them up from dealing with what is actually perfectly normal childhood behavior when faced with unrelenting boredom, so that the disciplinarian can concentrate on real misbehaviors like vandalism, the occasional fight, or the group of girls who always seem to smell like cigarettes.

Creating a Classroom Atmosphere: Part Three

Positive Discipline

There are three main reasons for keeping order in the class, which in turn keeps the loving, positive, and highly efficient learning environment intact, which is the whole point. Effective positive discipline protects the teacher from misbehaving students, students from misbehaving students, and misbehaving students from themselves.

We will start with protecting the role of teacher, from which all other good things will flow. The role of teacher is the most important civilizing force on the planet besides parent, and in the absence of any real parent becomes the central role in any society and should be respected as such. Period. A lot of things may be allowed in a classroom, but disrespect is not one of them. If a child yells out, "Hey, fatso, why don't you shut up, I'm trying to get some sleep here," what the teacher doesn't do is continue to teach. If the teacher continues to teach, there is no class. The teacher may think that they are educating, but nobody learns anything from whom they disrespect. If disrespect on any order of magnitude is not met immediately and effectively then your class will slip slide away from you. The teacher needs to remain rock solid for the sake of teachers and children everywhere. To be even more specific, some children come from homes where there is no functioning adult around that they respect or that can teach them respect, which will in turn enable them to grow up without respecting others or themselves. In short, as an adult, they are doomed. It is in these children that most disrespect will come and conversely it is for these children that it is highly important for the teacher to teach respect, for others at first, which can then be transferred to themselves as they learn how to act respectfully in their social relationships.

The Cultural Revolution in China had children dragging teachers out into the fields to work. I don't suggest this as a model for a modern school system. The Chinese do have an excellent proverb, however, that comes in handy. "The nail that sticks out the farthest is the one that gets hammered." In other words, don't be shocked by disrespect. There are an awful lot of dysfunctional homes out there and a poor economy is creating more daily. *Plan for disrespect* and have your disrespect guided missile on the launching pad and ready to go. The very second that something is said or done disrespecting the role of teacher, it is nail hammering time. If a thunderbolt shot out of the ceiling and a pile of smoldering ashes was to be seen in the chair of where a rude child once sat, the other children in the class are sure to notice. Not only notice but just maybe take a lesson from all of this so that it never happens again in that class, from anybody to anybody. So, make your individual disrespect plan really effective, and immediate. If you do, it will rarely ever have to be used. And, since you have preplanned all of this it can be done without anger and done in a positive tone so that it doesn't alienate any of the other children and keeps the loving atmosphere in the class intact, which has been temporarily soured by some sour behavior. What a teacher doesn't want to do is wait until they are really angry and then come up with a disrespect plan, because it doesn't usually go so well and yelling and screaming isn't much of a plan, anyway.

"Well, Steven, I can see that you have been studying vocabulary words. Unfortunately, none of those are on your word list, and at least three of them are illegal in most states. I am in a loving mood and will, in fact, save your life today. Because, you see (as you start dialing your phone), if I let you think that you can stand in the middle of a classroom and curse an adult you may grow up to think that this is acceptable behavior and will lose your valued career over something similar, and will grow up impoverished and bitter. And since I am a loving and caring man, I will not let this happen to you. "Yes, is this Mrs. Campbell? Yes, Ma'am, this is Mr. Hoatson. It is that time of year where I do home visits and discuss the career opportunities of my students with their parents so that they can succeed after they graduate. I like to discuss these things over dinner, so that it's relaxed and all of the family members can be in on the discussion. Yes, Ma'am tomorrow would be fine. Yes, I love chicken; that would be great. I'm looking forward to it. Oh, yes, I'm sure that Steven is looking forward to it, too. I've helped many young people prepare for the job world. It will be a pleasure." Click. Now, Steven is barely noticeable in his seat because he has shrunk to the size of a shriveled pea. He wishes that he was an invisible pea, but he is not. The children in the room who aren't laughing seem to be sitting up straighter in their seats than before. I can now bask in the glow of my fully restored loving atmosphere because I did nothing negative except give a child a very good education that day. So, be proactive, firm, loving, and brutally effective. Plan for disrespect, then work your plan, whatever it may be. If a respectful tone is set from day one, you don't have to worry much about day two or three. There are not many of Steven's classmates who are aspiring to be a shriveled pea.

POSITIVE DISCIPLINE: The art of saying positive things in the face of negative student behaviors to create a positive behavioral change. This could be the hardest thing in the world to do if you are angry, but I learned the power of this over years of living in Misbehavior, USA, more commonly referred to as a school. The foundation is set by knowing your students and knowing what makes them get out of bed in the morning. "What do you want to do when you grow up?" should be asked of any child that you come in contact with, whether three years old or seventeen. Get an answer. Hemming and hawing doesn't count. I don't care if the answer is to be a millionaire football player and the kid only weighs twenty pounds, take them at their word if they, in their own head, really mean it. It will dawn upon them later that a 300 lb. man chasing them down like the Giant going berserk after Jack is discovered fleeing down the bean stalk is kind of scary. Later that same child may answer "dentist." It doesn't particularly matter what career they chose. The girl that can barely read and hates school may say "doctor." Fine. Go with it. All the time. When you are disciplining you go straight to the child's own positive and use it when she is acting negatively. The teacher may even use the same tonal inflection that they would use when they are angry, because staring at ridiculous and uncalled for behavior tends to do that to one, but *it is the words that you use that count as far as actually changing the child's behavior in a positive way.* "John, you idiot, leave Larry alone. You're the meanest child I've ever seen. There is a jail cell with your name on it somewhere. Why don't you practice for it? Go to the office right now and spend a couple of days in ISS. Don't talk back to me. Make it a week." If John is found in the teacher's parking lot later in the day, it probably is to flatten some tires. Or, the teacher can try dealing with John another way. "John, what are you doing to Larry? Come here for a second, please. Listen, I'm not going to bite you, I've already had lunch. Come here, please. Now, look, you know I love you all day long, but you can't be putting your hands on people like that. And you know it. Do you realize that if you put your hands on the coach like that, your NBA career would be over? I'm serious. You would have flushed millions of dollars down the toilet in the blink of an eye. You've got to learn to control yourself, like for real. Now go apologize to Larry and shake his hand. I don't care if he did call you a chimpanzee. There is never any excuse for putting your hands on somebody, which, by the way, in the real world, is called assault and battery." Now it's the teachers turn to deal with big mouth Larry. It does indeed take two to Tango. "Yo, Dr. Doolittle, come up here for a second please. Yes, Larry, now would be nice. Auto mechanics make around thirty five dollars an hour, am I correct? Not bad for a young man like yourself. And they work with hard metallic tools like big, heavy wrenches, am I correct? So, I can assume that when you turn to the sweating, tired and grumpy hard working mechanic next to you and call him a chimpanzee that he is going to beat your brains in with whatever tool happens to be handy. The real question is why you think you can earn $35 an hour in the hospital?" Now, after shaking hands and class returns to normal, if either of these young men are found later in the day in the teacher's parking lot, it is probably to wash and wax the their teacher's car. Positive discipline flows from a teacher's strong sense of self and purpose in class coupled with a love for their children and a wish for their children to succeed all wrapped around the concept that if a child doesn't feel attacked, there is nothing to defend. If they do feel attacked, they will spend all of their energies into defending whatever crazy thing they just did, which means no behavioral change. If the child's positive self-image is brought into the picture, such as his career choice, then the child will gravitate to defending his positive image, which may just mean that he has to change his behavior. And they may just do so, if the positive atmosphere remains consistent. This is teaching and classroom control at a high level.

I'm going to take it to an even higher level. When a teacher is dealing with children who have had a lot of negative experiences, more negativity is not going to help that child. They have to respond to life in all kinds of negative ways, almost all counterproductive, but they can't help themselves because there is very little self-control, just negative reaction after negative reaction. Most children would not think for one second that seriously injuring or killing someone because they accidentally got bumped into in the hall is a real option for a response. It can't be found anywhere on their radar screen. But there are some children where, to them, fighting is an option for almost anything, including "Why are you looking at me?" These are the children who need a positive discipline response the most. It may very well, in a very real sense, save their lives. It also may help turn them into a productive citizen instead of a time bomb.

As a teacher, train yourself always to be positive in negative situations, especially when the natural response would be to get very angry. Another phrase for anger is losing one's temper, which translates into losing control of yourself and the situation, which means that nobody is in control of the negative situation, except anger itself, with its ugly brother, violence, lurking in the shadows somewhere, always ready to come to anger's aid. Now, I've said before that I have broken up a lot of fights, but I have never been the object of that fight. And I have diffused many before they even start, which is way better. It is all in how the teacher carries himself and what, in the child's mind, that teacher stands for. If you have created the proper loving atmosphere in the class and established the proper caring relationship with child and parent, you have set yourself up to do some real good in troubled children's lives. Troubled children need to see positive reactions to life situations SOMEWHERE, because they obviously haven't seen it much from their surrounding adults or larger community or they wouldn't be reacting negatively to every little thing in their lives. They need a positive role model which often means YOU, the teacher. So, model it up. Find your own way, and model like you're on the cover of Vogue.

I worked with teenagers at a place where they were sent instead of being expelled from school and would be confronted on a daily basis with how to manage angry people who weren't doing so well. I would enter a classroom if called, look at the young man involved in whatever nonsense it was and start with, "You know I love you, man. You know I do, and I know that you are going to be a great fill in the blank career, but we can't have this, and you know it. Come on with me and let's figure this out." And they would come. The first time that a thug wannabe hears that they are loved, especially coming out of the mouth of a grown man, they will probably howl in laughter or stare at you in disbelief, trying to figure out if you mean love or sex. They often get offended because they think you mean sex because they have had very little experience with being loved, which is why they want to be a thug in the first place, to put that armor plating on that is desperately needed to protect a broken child. After a while, though, I would enter a room and be greeted by a chorus of "We love you Mr. Hoatson" along with the laughter, and I would respond with a deep sniffing of the air, "Yes, I feel the love in the air. It is a beautiful day and we are blessed to be alive. Now, Frederick, please put the teacher down and follow me, because your career game plan is going south quickly. And pull up your pants. People will see the hearts on your underwear." As I would leave with surly Frederick I would be getting high fives from the other gentlemen in the class. "Train him up, Mr. H", "Show him the love." And I would do both.

A note on troubled girls: Many of them have come from harsh environments with little love also, but are constantly seeking it. Some are seeking male approval from a father they never knew. Unfortunately, in the search for some kind of real love, they run into a constant bombardment of the cheap love substitute, sex. It is just as important for them to feel the real, caring love from a good teacher, as it is for the boys. But, just as the boys have to be disabused of the notion that their physical strength is their real power, girls have got to get it out of their heads that their physical beauty is their real power source. If the teacher wants to have a for real STUDENT in their class, the girl has got to think of her brain and depth of character as her power source. So, when I am dealing with an unruly girl who is a little too full of her teenage self and dresses at school like its amateur night at the strip club, it would go something like this. "Elizabeth, come up here, for a second please. Because I asked you to, that's why. I heard some kind of a vicious rumor that you stole something from the store the other day. Yes, I know that the world is full of lying haters but this hater happens to be your mother. Let me clue you in on something. If you ever get caught shoplifting, your dreams of becoming a nurse will be gone . . . forever. You might be able to get a job selling hamburgers, but that is not a sure bet because those companies frown on stealing, also. It's something silly about their profit margin. You have way too much talent to waste it on stupidity. You will be saving people's lives in a nurse's uniform. Respect that, and yourself. Speaking of respect, nurses don't dress like that. I've seen more clothes on people taking a shower. Put some clothes on, girl. And steal a better shade of lipstick. Neon purple doesn't sit well with the heart patients. It could trigger something."

Positive discipline: It works all day long, and it's cheaper than blood pressure medicine, because the teachers are not finding themselves in the middle of unpleasant confrontations. It also allows positive classroom atmospheres to be restored quickly. It also establishes that the teacher is in complete charge of her emotions and the classroom, which is very comforting to children, all the more so to children that come from backgrounds where there are no adults really in charge, no real role models.

The second reason for strong positive discipline in the classroom is to protect the role of the student for each child. In other words, protect children from each other. <u>The Lord of the Flies </u>is not a model for a safe learning environment. If "Let's get Piggy!" rings out from the back of the class, Zeus, the teacher, needs to start flinging lightning bolts immediately, so that this never happens again. In a safe learning atmosphere, meaning one where a child's scholastic efforts are never ridiculed but encouraged, a child is never shamed, but supported. It is important for every child to thrive, but *vital for the struggling student.*

Some children have a steel-strong sense of self, are comfortable with their intellectual abilities, and are impervious to name calling by other students. The teacher doesn't have to worry about them being bullied. If a child hurls an insult at them, they would respond with, "Listen, I'm going to be a brain surgeon in twenty years and judging from how yours appears to be malfunctioning right now, you might very well be a patient of mine. My suggestion is that you shut up so that I can concentrate over here and pray that I have learned enough when your time comes. And that I don't slip." Insults will bounce off of a child that feels secure with herself.

An insecure child, one that can't read very well and views reading out loud as a humiliating chore, or views math as deciphering confusing hieroglyphics, is a whole different animal entirely. They have no emotional armor to protect themselves, because their own self-view is really shaky. So, if a truly struggling child is insulted, his response is not going to be cool calm and collected. It will range anywhere from locking himself in the bathroom and blubbering like a baby to launching himself and his newly sharpened pencil like a hate-seeking missile to do some lesson teaching of his own.

No matter what the response, all academically floundering children have one thing in common: if they are attacked for asking a question that somebody else deems is stupid, or gives an answer that is considered a 10 on the lame scale, you can bet a dollar that they will cease doing either. They will ask no questions or give no answers, because that is WAY too risky. They will clam up and work on creating their own internal pearls for the rest of the year, because it is safe in their shells. Their stock in trade will be "I don't know" which means "Leave me alone, you're freaking me out." "Oh, come on Iris, you've done this type of problem before, give it a try for all the world to see." The teacher will get, "I REALLY don't know" now because Iris is aware that Marcela, who has watched every episode of "Mean Girls" three times just to make sure that she didn't miss anything, is eyeballing her suspiciously. "Leave me alone" is the kiss of death for any struggling child, academically, emotionally, or lost at sea. "Leave me alone" means that these children will be reading on the grade level at which they were abandoned for the rest of their lives. Their math skills will be frozen in time, which is not good if they can't even give the correct change.

As the child grows older and the gap between what they should know and what they actually do know grows wider and wider, the humiliation factor gets exponentially bigger and bigger if they are ever found out. At this stage every bit of intellectual energy is diverted from actually learning anything new to protecting themselves from being discovered that they can actually do very little. Eventually the children become young adults and find themselves lost.

True story: I was going to buy a couple of dogwood trees from a small nursery near the high school where I taught. A seventeen year old girl who was a student at the school was at the cash register and was the only staff at the nursery until the boss got back. I walked up to Linda, trees in hand, and gave her a cheery "Hello." She wasn't cheery. She looked worried and confused. "What's the matter?" "The cash register is broken. I can get the money and all, but it won't work. I don't know what to do." It became evident that although she knew the concept of adding, she didn't know how to give change or figure sales tax, or, if figured, to add it to the total to get the proper amount. She was scared and her eyes were beginning to well up with tears. "What are you going to do? There are other adults in here who are going to want to buy something." "I don't know, Mr. Hoatson," was the response and her tears started to flow. I took her by the chin. "Look at me. You can do this. I am going to give you a crash course in basic math and you are going to learn this quickly, because you are a smart girl." She nodded her head. We found a calculator in a drawer, and a receipt book and she paid real, real close attention and she survived the next two hours. Teachers and bureaucrats can cluck their tongues all they want about what a failure this girl is and ask why in the world didn't she know anything beyond third grade math? They can even go out and find somebody to punish for this travesty, but the fact of the matter is this poor girl should never have been put in this position. I can tell you why this child and all the other children like her are thrust into positions that they are wholly unqualified for, and that is because somewhere along the line their classroom experiences became negative and the classroom became a fearful place. They went deep inside a shell to protect themselves and never came out because they didn't feel that it was safe. It may feel safe inside the shell, but absolutely no learning will take place in there. Hiding and exploring are not synonymous. The parent better hope that it is an oyster-type shell that their child is hiding in, so that maybe they will be working on producing pearls. *Don't EVER let another child pick on, crack on, make fun of, ridicule or put down another child because those that aren't doing so well will flee to the interior regions of their minds and not pop up again until they are skill-less, clueless, adults.* In fact, the main role of a loving and safe classroom atmosphere, enforced by iron positive discipline, is to protect struggling children in their endeavors to get competent and through competence, develop a sense of internal strength, which will carry them through life's tough times. Once their internal self-view is one of competence and confidence, they can deal with stupidity coming from others without clamming up, and continue on their merry way pursuing their education. From a child's point of view, the most important thing that happens at school is not necessarily to get an education, but to avoid humiliation and shame. Ask any child who has had a truly bad haircut what he is thinking about at his desk. There isn't one in a thousand that would say "my lesson." This is a good lesson for all teachers to keep in mind.

The other thing for teachers to keep in mind is that a child asking a question or willing to give an answer that may not be correct in front of their peers is an act of bravery and should be rewarded. Reading out loud in class, which is absolutely necessary for maximum reading growth, is the perfect example of where a positive atmosphere is not only necessary, but really helpful. Once you have established a routine where children can stumble and bumble and receive nothing but praise from teacher and peers, you have a real educational machine going. "Great job Jesse, much smoother." "Do it Luis, do it. You are a reading machine." "Go Emma go. Go Emma go." Now, all this was said to kids who were stinking it up during reading, creating joy out of struggle. As the teacher praises, one eye is always cocked and loaded, staring at the class wise guys in a "don't you dare" fashion, in which case they probably won't. Once a pleasant and safe atmosphere becomes a routine, it becomes a self-generating engine of learning, because everybody is getting pleasure out of it. Even the class wise guys don't like getting ridiculed and feel better about the class. They are often wise guys because it is better in their mind to strike first. Their ridicule is a preemptive attempt to ward off what they think is eventually coming towards them. If no ridicule ever shows up in the classroom, just kids having fun learning, there is no longer a need to be a wise guy as a defense mechanism.

I would openly set up the "no ridicule" rule from the first day and give an historical setting for it. "The entire human race was plunged into a world war many years ago because some members of the human race had the arrogance and audacity to think that they were SUPERIOR to everybody else and thus had the right to do whatever they wished to others who they deemed inferior. Thank goodness we live in a land where all men and women are created equal, and under law have equal rights to life, liberty and the pursuit of happiness. Since this is an American classroom we have the right to have a free and happy education, particularly being free of some arrogant children who have the bigoted and evil notion that they are superior to others, and thus think that they can say and do bad things to whomever they deem inferior. It is great to be in a classroom where I know for a fact that false notions of superiority don't reside in any of my students, and who will show their depth of respect for the American way of life by treating others as equals and letting them pursue their quest for education and happiness without dipping into their business as they read or do math and/or any other lessons by making negative or disparaging remarks. If I sense a child who thinks in his own mind that he is superior to all others, I will immediately visit that child's parents to see if they have indeed spawned a superior life form to the rest of us human beings, because if so, government scientists should be notified immediately. Do we understand each other?" As the teacher asks this the roving teacher eye will make full eye contact with the child or two that does, indeed, have the bad habit of making fun of others, to plumb the depths of their understanding. When they nod their heads, the teacher may continue with the process of education, including reading out loud. Every child is now free and clear to learn to the best of his or her ability without fear, which is the "learn to the best of their ability" killer.

The third reason for strong positive discipline in the classroom is to protect the misbehaving children from themselves. Over time, all behaviors become habit forming. If a child has a habit of being rude, disrespectful or violent, these are not going to do him or her in good stead when they become an adult. It is imperative that these bad habits are squeezed out of them and replaced by good ones such as politeness, respect, and constructive, nonviolent behavior as early as possible. One of the main functions of a classroom is to teach civilizing attitudes and habits to ensure a decent society. That will be found in the fine print on your college diploma somewhere. Many young adults have a hard time finding gainful employment, not because they are academically deficient, but because they are socially deficient. "Can you please show me where the shoe department is?" "Bump you, I'm busy!" is not a good response. The classroom is the perfect incubator for modeling and practicing good, positive behaviors. The earlier the better. Keep in mind that the socializing incubator at that child's home or community may be broken. If a misbehaving child learns how to act in positive ways in a classroom, the teacher has given that child skills to succeed as an adult that, in many ways, are a lot more important than whatever academics they may have learned. Every child who learns to act in a positive, constructive manner in school is an adult in the making that can be a positive contributor to society. Not only does it make our country a better place to live, but is cheaper than flushing $10-20,000 down a rat hole to house dysfunctional people in a cage for a year. Every single person in prison is a teacher's aide or a half of a teacher taken out of the picture, not to mention a life and talent wasted. Loving, efficient and positively ordered classrooms can be game changers for struggling children. Teachers, you are more important than you think.

Part Four:
The Nuts and Bolts of
Successful Teaching

Every single thing that I am going to say here is probably intuitive to a lot of teachers, but is absolutely counterintuitive to the educational powers that be because most schools are set up to do the exact opposite of what it takes to help struggling children succeed in school. Schools are set up to punish slow learners and struggling students and the teachers who teach them in a vain and backwards attempt to get children to do better on tests. I am going to assume that these people who make bad school policy are not evil, but simply don't know what they are doing. I don't think that they understand children very well. *I am going to describe precisely how to get the best out of children and am coming from the point of view that if they are absorbing and applying information as efficiently as their brain will let them, they are doing the best they can and that is all that can be asked of any child!* You cannot ask any more from children than to do their best. I don't care what anybody else thinks about what that child should be capable of, including some who live in a fantasy world where continuously "raising the bar" and artificially pressuring children and teachers to reach said bar seems like a good idea. Not only is this NOT a good idea, but creates such an unpleasant atmosphere for children who aren't doing well in school that they will go Huckleberry Finn on you and light out for a life on the raft. Check out the dropout rates and the home schooling rates sometime. There are a whole lot of children who have fled the public school system in one way or another, and many of those are the very ones that need to be in a school the most. It is a cold world out there for the skill-less. I am also coming from the point of view that ALL of the children who are sent to a teacher are a blessing and it is the teacher's job to ensure that ALL are doing the best that they can. That is the very definition of a well-run classroom. We've already created the loving atmosphere for this to happen. Now let's put into practice some ideas that will ensure that each child does his best.

The first thing is to understand brain function. There are seven different kinds of intelligence and everybody's brain is strong in some areas and weaker in others. That's why some people can fix a transmission with their eyes closed, but your pediatrician can't because he is an idiot around cars. And don't have your mechanic try to deliver your baby. Some children can read like a bird sings, but figuring out how to balance a check book is almost impossible. "Don't worry Mr. Hoatson, I'll just use cash." Yeah, right. "You better buy an armored car to transport your house payment." Not only are children strong and weak in different areas, but the amount of new information that a child can absorb in an hour or a day is different. In preschool, some children can sit raptly as the teacher reads War and Peace, while others have checked out of this rapt attention thing before you can say, "Henny Penny went to the barnyard." They can be found over by the blocks building bridges. Or knocking down other's bridges. Whatever. Besides the amount of information that can be absorbed per hour, there is the rate at which information can be absorbed, which is different for everybody. If you want to check out your own brain absorption rate go take piano lessons for the first time. While you are at it, see if it is helpful that the teacher looks thoroughly disgusted at the end of your practice session and marks your bill with an emphatic bright red "F" before he hands it to you. What all of this points to, is that, you don't need to raise the bar on children because each child has her own individual, internal bar that she will happily raise every single day, if the experience is pleasant. The other thing about the brain is that it naturally likes learning. That is what it does. That is its biological function. You don't have to force a brain to learn any more than you have to force a stomach to digest food or an eye to see. If a brain is learning it is in its natural state, thus happy. It doesn't really matter WHAT it is learning. If it is digesting new things, it is happy. A case in point is my good neighbor Bob. He is fascinated by things that I have absolutely no interest in whatsoever. I don't care a single thing about my lawnmower except that it runs. If it doesn't I call Bob. Bob will go into detail about what a certain part does as he is dealing with what is basically owner neglect. He will eventually get to the owner neglect part, but before that I am fascinated by his grasp of physics and why certain parts do certain things, because he explains things so that I can comprehend what is going on and I am actually learning something. Now, after he has chastised me for being an idiot and left for home, I am not going to run to a book on lawn mower parts and read up on it more, because, like I said, I couldn't care less. But while my brain was temporarily learning something new I wasn't bored. I was fascinated. *You do not have to force real learning, just set up situations where real learning will take place in the classroom.*

First Helpful Classroom Tip: *Do no harm.* I know that this is the first rule of thumb for the medical profession, but I am going to steal it and say that it should be emblazoned on every school wall. When a child boldly states, "I don't like history," or science or math or my personal favorite "I don't like to read," it is time for everybody to take three large steps back and ask, "How in the world is that actually possible?" It is even more imperative to ask that question if a child adds extra emphasis to his negative view of learning, such as "I hate math" or "Reading makes me puke." How is this possible? It's because someone made learning, which is a natural function, really, really unpleasant. There is no other possible explanation. And there is no excuse for it, either. Let us look at other natural functions that should be pleasant. Eating ice cream is one. If a person was force fed a pint of blueberry ice cream every half hour for a year, that person probably would never eat anything with the word "berry" in it ever again, and would probably repaint any room of the house that even resembled a shade of blue. Sex should be pleasant enough, except that there is an entire industry built on helping people who have had negative experiences with it. Anything can be made so unpleasant that a person wants to avoid it at all costs, including learning. Do no harm. Every teacher. Every school.

Second Helpful Classroom Tip: The heck with grades, *reward effort.* I was teaching writing to exceptional education 10th graders years ago when I got a new student who had just transferred from another school. She, like most of my students when I first get them, couldn't write her way out of a paper bag. The spelling of "bag" may have been problematic. I have my students write every day, which she wasn't used to because evidently her school was a large fan of ditto sheets. Anyway, I wrote three beginning sentences on the board and the students were to make them into a story. Some chose mystery, others comedy. Whatever suited them. Cheryl gave it her best shot. Her paper was terrible and she knew it. She was almost visibly trembling. As I walked among the students I stopped at her desk to see how she was doing. She looked up at me, started crying, and asked, "Do I get an "F"? "Why should you get an "F"? You're writing aren't you?" "Well, it's all wrong," she replied, trying not to cry too much in front of these strangers. "Sweetheart, the assignment wasn't to write a perfect paper. The assignment was to write a story the best you can out of one of these three sentences on the board, which you are in fact doing. This here is an "A" paper. At least it will be once we've made what looks to me like four thousand corrections on this thing. The story itself looks fine. I love murder mysteries." The girl was stunned. She had never gotten an "A" paper. She also stopped crying. "Now Carlos over here, who evidently went to an all-night party without inviting me, because he is drooling in his sleep, is flirting with an "F" because he is laying on a blank sheet of paper, which is the only way that it is remotely possible to get an "F" in my class. Got it?" A much brighter Cheryl nodded and actually smiled. I went over to Carlos to help him achieve his "A" for the day. "Hey, dream boy, wake it up. Your girlfriend called and said that if you go to sleep at school one more time that she is going to start dating Robert. I think she means it this time."

Reward effort all the time because if a child is trying to learn, even if the outcome is temporarily poor, he is doing his job as a student. Let me tell you something. Children who have had a series of failing experiences in the classroom are not made of stern stuff. More like Jello. They will crumble quickly when faced with difficult tasks. They have no resiliency to bounce back from mistakes, which they regard as signs of failure because they have been told that over and over and will internalize the fact that the only thing they are good at is failing. What you get is a tearful "Do I get an "F"? or sometimes a class clown or sometimes a bully or sometimes an empty seat. Every child will deal with failure in his own way. Don't let children feel that they are failures. Ever. Find a way to reward their efforts. Make their efforts pleasurable, because struggling through something that you are not very good at, like math is work. Work has got to be rewarded. Ask any employer how many employees they have that show up daily on a volunteer basis. Now, minimum wage employers may dream of workers working for free, they're almost there anyway. They have got to pay them something, albeit begrudgingly or else the parking lot will resemble a ghost town. So, reward your children's real efforts in the class, no matter if the science paper looks like it was written by Einstein's great grandson or by an orangutan that happened to find a pen lying on the ground. Have faith in the child. Have faith in the fact that if children are really trying, that eventually they will get to a higher level of academic performance, no matter how woeful their performances may seem today. The brain is automatically going to perform mental tasks better if it keeps trying those tasks repeatedly. If a person sticks with piano lessons long enough, what comes out of that piano may be something that approaches enjoyable. Just keep trying and don't get discouraged. That is the attitude the teacher wants from her student. What the teacher doesn't want for a child to do is shut down, which is exactly what Cheryl would have done if I had answered her question "Do I get an "F"?" with a "Yes."

Third Helpful Classroom Tip: *Success breeds success.* The straight "A" students in a school have no problem with this concept, because they have success experiences daily in class. Sometimes hourly. The failing child, the one who everybody from the janitor to the superintendent of schools is praying feverishly will do better on her tests, doesn't have a clue how to spell success, much less what it really means. Knowing what success feels like is imperative to actually succeeding, because it takes a lot more than just knowing subject matter to be a success in the classroom or in life. I have watched a lot of sports teams that have a lot of physical talent but for some odd reason always fall short when it comes to actually winning in a consistent manner. This is one of the reasons that I don't bet on sports. I may love that team and everybody on it but they are lacking something that keeps them from succeeding. One of the things that they are lacking is an actual feel for what it is like to be a winner. On the other hand, there are teams out there that you know are going to win the game just by the way they swagger out onto the field. The team is down by a zillion points and the coach can be seen calmly picking his teeth with a toothpick while he works his way out of another tight spot, which he has done a million times before, and finds a way, AGAIN, to send the other team home crying like babies. Winning is a mental attitude, a toughness that only comes with overcoming adversity and dealing with failure.

It comes from working through unpleasant and painful situations, because in one's mind's eye the pain will be worth it if you win. The only way that you can know that is if you have actually won. There are other teams that, bless them, seem to find creative ways to not win, but lose. In their mind's eye they are losers and can't quite shake the feeling that something bad is going to happen and when faced with adversity, instead of digging in with granite determination to win, their mind is thinking, "Oh, oh, here we go again."

"Oh, oh, I'm going to fail again," is the mindset of any child who has a history of failures. This is not a mindset conducive to raising test scores and saving everybody's paycheck. The struggling child needs a series of successful experiences to internalize what success feels like. This is the teacher's main job; to set struggling children up for success experiences. Daily. Hourly. Set them up so that the failing child is replaced by one that has a positive, "I can do this" self-view and one that has the mental toughness to deal with difficulty, because the child KNOWs that he can succeed. The teacher is going to have to actively, consciously build a successful child.

First, find where the child's success level really is. Hide the grade book and erase any concept of grading and find out what that child in front of you can actually, really, do. It doesn't matter that the child is fifteen and is supposed to be reading on a tenth grade level. If the best she can do is read <u>Betty, the Fluffy Yellow Duck</u> well, that is her success level. Don't freak out, just go there and build her up from there. I would keep several different levels of books in my desk and have each child read from each one until

I could tell where their abilities lie. If a child is stumbling over more than a word or two per couple of sentences, enough so that she couldn't actually get a reading rhythm going, I would back it up until she could read fairly fluently. This is her success level. I would build from that by getting increasingly harder books that would be read until fluency and keep on going. If children are having a good time and are praised, not punished, for their work, their reading or math levels will rise like the Phoenix. Have faith in the brain to do its job. It will. Did I mention hide the grade book? The only thing that a struggling child needs to hear is "good job" and sometimes, "really, really good job." Then there is, "Whoa, hoss, I can't believe what I'm hearing. It's like angels singing. Let's get your dad on the phone and you read this to him right now. Here, you dial it. I'm feeling faint." If a struggling child gets enough success experiences, you don't have a struggling child anymore. Now, sixteen year old boys would rather put their hand in a wood chipper than read <u>Betty, the Fluffy Yellow Duck</u> so age appropriate material is important. It's out there, at all levels.

Teaching math is easier than teaching reading, because finding a child's skill level is easy if you pay attention to what he is doing. If a child blows a division problem badly, check out why. Can he multiply? Can he subtract? Can he add? If he can do all that, then he just doesn't understand the process. Find where a child is shaky, step back a bit to his success level, then build.

There is another kind of success level that I try to find in each child and that is their *understanding level.* Just because children get a right answer doesn't mean that they know what they are doing. An ape can follow a repairman around with a screwdriver all day long, but it doesn't mean he knows what to do with it. To check understanding, just ask some questions and whatever you do DON'T call on the child who always raises her hand to answer. Ask the child hiding in the back row in a futile attempt to be invisible. "All right, Sonya, I've got 4/5 of a desk. What the heck does that five mean?" If she can't tell you that some nut snuck in and carved your desk into five pieces and then had the courtesy to leave you four, there is a problem. "This guy is hitting with a .125 batting average. Should he be made team captain or shipped out to the Siberia farm club?" ""Which is bigger, .1 or .0999?" "Which would you rather have, 1/4 of a pizza or 25%?" "What is the real price if it is 35% off?" In discussing the civil war and the importance of the Dred Scott decision and the Missouri compromise, mathematics are involved in deciphering murky Supreme Court decisions. Far reaching questions can be asked, such as, "What is up with this 3/4 of a man declaration, what does he look like and does he stand a chance of getting a date?" In science, one of my favorites is "When you go outside at night and you see all of those stars, what are you really looking at? What is a star?" Depending on the grade level you would be amazed at the creativity and wrongness of the answers. So, find a child's understanding level as well as his success level and just keep on building on those. Always teach to understanding. Skills are fine, but should lead children to a deeper understanding of what they are doing. If children don't truly understand what they are doing, but can mimic the skills involved, then their foundation is built on sand and will collapse later. I have found that most of the time when a child is confused about something today, it is because of a very shaky understanding of what happened previously. The teacher has to become Sherlock Holmes and go into the past to figure out where the child fell off the train, teach to understanding that puts the child back on the train, and then bring her back to the station. If a teacher is constantly checking for a deep understanding of a subject, it creates a mental foundation for a child that is built on concrete instead of sand and will not collapse on down the line when the child has to grapple with something new. It also cuts way down on the amount of backward time traveling that a teacher has to do, which can be exhausting. The more children succeed and are rewarded for it, the more success becomes a habit, and the more they will learn. They will stop wasting their energies on avoiding school work, because success feels good, freeing up their mental energy to learn. Now you have a real student sitting in front of you.

Fourth helpful classroom tip: *Don't Punish Mistakes, Correct Them.* The funny thing about Cheryl and all the other kids who couldn't write worth a lick is that over time they learned to write fairly well; some of them quite well. They did so because I never punished them for mistakes, in a judgmental sense. No "F"s or "D"s or frowny faces; just plain, cold, nonjudgmental corrections. Write, correct, rewrite. Always with a "good job" remark if they were trying their best.

The plain fact of the matter is that rewriting is work that everybody wants to avoid, so the child's brain will automatically learn the rules of English as fast as possible to avoid laborious rewriting. I learned this the hard way once, when I was possessed by the delusion that I was a novelist. My editor handed back to me what I had supposed was a near perfect manuscript. It was, in fact, 500 pages of red correction marking that had to be redone, line by painful line. Amidst my sobbing, I learned a couple of things about writing. Write and rewrite will produce better writing. Write and be punished for it will produce something else. If a child is simply correcting mistakes without any judgment, the teacher doesn't have to deal with the blank sheet of paper syndrome. Some children are so afraid of being "wrong" that they will freeze up and simply do nothing. They are avoiding the shame of failure by the fact that they haven't done anything to fail at. Of course, they have learned absolutely nothing, but that is not the child's main concern. It may be teacher's main concern, but not the child's. The child's main concern is to not look like a fool in front of his peers.

To take this up a notch, if punishment for effort is not only taken out of the picture, but instead a chance to look like a hero in front of one's peers is added, the teacher has set up a genuine opportunity for maximum effort and learning. Every Friday in writing class was "Showtime." I would sit at my desk, clear my throat, and read the best of the weekly writings. I would not identify the authors, but they could identify themselves with a gleeful "That was mine!" if they felt like it. They would hoot and howl and laugh and sometimes nod somberly in approval if somebody had veered off into a heavy subject, but did it well. The power of peer approval for intellectual endeavors cannot be overstated. Sometimes the only peer approval they get is in stupidity contests such as who can chug-a-lug the most alcohol out in the woods when the adults aren't looking. If effort is not only not punished, but rewarded by peer approval you will get maximum, sometimes high quality effort.

Why drama, art, music, industrial arts and home economics have been taken out of the school I don't know, but it borders on being criminal. I suggest that teachers make it real clear to anybody within earshot that they want all of this stuff back, because they are perfect vehicles for children to get praise by their peers for doing positive things. Plus, if you want parents to come to the school, ditch the deadly dull PTA meeting and have the children perform something. Anything. I am clearly drifting off the subject here, but I feel better. It is relevant in a tangential sense, however.

"You will get an "A" if you don't erase your mistakes," should be declared at the beginning of each and every math class. If the teacher doesn't say something like this the student will erase anything that remotely resembles a mistake. If a teacher punishes mistakes with bad grades or belittling comments, that is EXACTLY what any sane child will do. Erase them immediately before they are found out. They must do it slyly though, in case the class snitch ferrets them out and brings their miserable failure to the teacher's attention. Children have had it drilled into their heads that mistakes are bad. Since children want to please adults and don't want to be seen as bad, they will just pretend the mistake didn't happen. "I don't know how I came to the conclusion that two boxes of cereal would be $756, but look, my paper is mistake free, so everything is fine." It's fine for the school if they can sucker Johnny into buying from the school store.

Visible mistakes are a teacher's best friend because they are a window into the child's mind; his thinking process. If Johnny hadn't erased his shame, the terrible mistake that he had made, the teacher could have glanced down and quickly deduced that it was either a decimal point problem, or an addition problem, or a process problem such as not knowing how to carry, or an understanding problem such as multiplying instead of adding, or a reading problem of the problem, or simply that Johnny can't cheat very well off of his neighbor because he needs new glasses. Without a visible mistake to look at, the teacher knows NOTHING. With a visible mistake, a teacher knows all and sees all. An omniscient teacher is much better than the blind leading the blind. The only way to get to see mistakes on a paper is to drift far away from the idea that the classroom experience is for correct answers only, and set sail for the Isle of understanding instead. For a child to understand something deeply, mistakes will be made. Mistakes need to be judgment free, however, so that a child is willing to let learning take place in his head instead of hiding. To do this, set up a mistake loving environment. It should incorporate a rhythm, such as work, work, mistake, correct, understand, work, work, laugh at the mistake, learn from it, work, work. This is much better than what can often be found, which is: work, work, work, work, test, grade, find mistakes-lots of them, punish child, cry, cry, work, work, work.

Setting up a mistake loving classroom is easy. *The teacher just endorses the concept that it is through mistakes that real learning takes place* and imparts that concept to the student. "I have found in my study of science that many great discoveries have been the result of mistakes, mishaps and blunders. The reason why the stupid mistake turned into a truly great discovery is that the scientist didn't get all shook by it and run to the closet to suck his thumb. The scientist instead used the scientific method, which is "Holy mackerel that was dumb. I won't do THAT again. I'm lucky I wasn't killed," and carried on with his or her quest for greatness *by learning what he can from the mistake until he reaches his goal.* Penicillin would not have been discovered if the scientist searching for medicinal cures hadn't completely messed up by eating a sandwich over his Petri dishes, thus contaminating his entire experiment. Fortunately for him the bread was moldy and fortunately for the world this guy was smart enough to notice that the mold had killed a bunch of bacteria in the Petri dish. If he had tried to cover up his mistake because he was afraid of being fired for his incompetence, he would not have made his discovery.

Thomas Edison is the poster child for learning from mistakes. It took Edison over 900 attempts before he got the light bulb right. Over 900 mistakes. They would have been over 900 failures if he had internalized that view of what a mistake was, but he didn't. He viewed each mistake as a learning experience, and he mistaked his way to changing civilization forever. In the field of sports, it is not the athlete who plays perfectly that drives a team to victory, it is the person who is not rattled by a serious mistake, learns from it immediately, and focuses intently under pressure to succeed. These types of athletes are even more dangerous after having really messed up, because their focus on winning becomes laser-like, which enhances their efforts toward winning. So, teachers, hide the grade book for a while, like maybe in an Indiana Jones type of inaccessible place and let children learn from their mistakes because they will feel free to do so. It will enhance their efforts to succeed because they won't freeze up like a deer in the headlights every time they encounter something that they are not sure of. If a child is sitting, trembling, and staring motionless at her blank sheet of paper for long periods of time, this is not a good sign. If Edison did that we would still be groping around in the dark searching for the candle we just dropped.

Fifth helpful classroom tip: *Burn your desk and learn the power of proximity.* Well, don't actually burn the desk, just get away from it 99.99999999% of the time. Do not sit behind your desk and wait for the children to mess up and then get all mad about it. Head the messing up part off at the pass. Constantly walk around the room, back and forth, up and down, around and around. Do not follow the model of the teacher who is covered in barnacles. Move. For starters, it's good exercise. Nothing wrong with that. But beyond that, constantly being in contact with the children, both visually and physically, reaps unbelievable rewards that you can't even fathom if you remain anchored in one spot.

Reward one: *The teacher's misbehavior problems virtually disappear,* because every few minutes the teacher is physically hovering over each child, like a hawk over a field of mice, except REAL CLOSE. The mouse won't even squeak, much less steal cheese with the hawk eyeballing it six inches away. There is not a child in his right mind that would act up with the teacher one inch away. This circulating by the teacher is done in a loving and friendly way, but just the fact of physical proximity creates better behavior automatically, without anybody really noticing it. The children don't notice they are being controlled, because while the teacher is circulating she is constantly teaching one on one as she spots problems. Instead of grading, which entails both rewards and punishment; she is simply being HELPFUL, all day long. Her close physical presence is not seen as a threat, but as a pleasure, because it means that help is always on the way. Since children feel free to ask questions in a classroom with a loving atmosphere, they are constantly asking and receiving help, which creates constant upward learning.

Reward Two: *The mistakes made by children drop like a rock, because they are being corrected as soon as they are made.* I have never understood the teaching model of letting children make lots of mistakes, over and over again, until they become ingrained as bad habits, and then punishing them for it with bad grades. Even worse is continuing to do this with another set of skills. There is absolutely no time allowed to go back and meticulously break the child of the bad habits that the teacher allowed to develop in the first place. Undoing a bad habit is three times as taxing as it is to teach something correctly in the first place. I think that some policy makers need to look into who spiked their water coolers and take immediate action. Some children struggle a lot in school and it is less than helpful to them to be allowed to constantly flounder and blunder their way through the day and then tell them as the sun is going down that they are not doing so well. The teacher knew that before the sun even came up. The best way to help that child is not to let them flounder and blunder in the first place. As the teacher is in motion and passes a struggling child's desk, he points out helpful things right then and there. "Look at that, Jaden. Your character is talking here but doesn't say "she said", so you don't put the quotation mark here. It just goes around what they actually say, which would be over here." "Okay." Then the teacher strolls on his merry way. The teacher might even throw in an enlightening example, such as, "Jaden, if I wrote, "Fernando, sit down quickly because you are bothering everybody yelled Mr. Hoatson with steam coming out of his ears," where would the quotation marks go?" Jaden would actually be able to tell where the quotation marks went because she has learned something. What the teacher didn't do was let Jaden write a five page story with 400 misplaced quotation marks, scold her for it, punish her for it, and then give her another five page assignment to do on the joys of writing.

If a teacher is strolling, checking and correcting during a math assignment, there is a world of difference between catching a student in mid-mistake or correcting them after they have made a sea of mistakes. If Mrs. McGrath noticed that Thomas was having trouble with addition, she could point out that carrying goes to the left and not the right, explain why, and then have Thomas do a couple of problems correctly. She could end with, "Good work Thomas. You are a genuine human adding machine," and watch the boy giggle and glow. If Mrs. McGrath didn't want to correct mistakes immediately, she could always approach Thomas the traditional way. "What the heck is this? You did all 2,500 problems wrong and are going to have to redo them all. I've told you a million times that you carry to the left, to the left, do you hear? We don't have time for this now. Do them during lunch. By the way, you get an "F". Thomas #1 learned how to add properly. Thomas #2 learned how to hate Mrs. McGrath and math all in one fell swoop.

I will tell you right now, teaching is not for the lazy. Constantly moving and answering what seems like hundreds of individual questions per hour, will drain you by the end of the day. The tradeoff is that the day is really pleasant and rewarding. It is worth the trade off, because if teachers are in constant punishment mode, they will find themselves not only equally drained, but the day itself will be full of unpleasantness and is considerably less rewarding. They may begin viewing being a greeter at a big box store as a viable alternative.

The people who gain from a roaming, constantly helping, constantly correcting, constantly loving teacher are the children. They are allowed to learn at their optimum learning rate and are not being put in the position of being exposed to a lot of failure experiences and negative social experiences daily. Success breeds success.

One more thought on failure experiences, and mistakes becoming ingrained as bad habit. I have second thoughts about homework. Third, fourth and fifth thoughts, too. Giving homework is tricky business, depending on the home and upon the work. What I worry about is that some homes don't provide a very good intellectual support system for the student. Some don't even provide a very good emotional or physical support system, either. There are a LOT of stressed homes out there, thanks in large part to the pyramid scheme of an economy that has evolved in this country. Sending homework that a child can't really do very well into a home that is headed by an overworked parent, who might not have the time or ability to help them, is counterproductive. If a child flounders and makes mistakes for a couple of hours with nobody there to correct anything or act as a guide, what the child is actually learning is how to flounder and make mistakes real well. Not only do bad habits become ingrained, but the negative experiences of being confused and performing poorly at a task are damaging to a child and impact how he does in the classroom. Additionally, the emotional damage done by parents being mad at the child at home because of poor performance, coupled with the frustration built up in the parent that can't really help the child out in any meaningful way because maybe they weren't Captain Whiz-bang at school either, makes me question whether or not any of this is helpful to a child who academically struggles at school. What is the point, exactly?

If a child can't really do the assignment in class, why send it home to do have it done even more poorly? If a child can do it in class, why send a boatload of repetitions home that steal time away from the family? Part of the reason that I learned to teach, walk, correct, encourage, teach, walk and correct, is that at the end of the hour I knew that all of the work had not only been done, but done correctly. I got a solid hour of good work out of the children. If I expect this to be done at the house, I have no idea if the work is going to be done right, or if at all. I have no control over the atmosphere in that household, whether that child is being praised for trying or beaten or yelled at because they weren't trying hard enough. Children who come from homes steeped in negativity don't need the school to inject a healthy dose of it into the household as well. I am not saying that homework is necessarily bad; I'm saying that it really needs to be thought through before it is given because it can often do more harm than good. As a teacher, I didn't want to take a bunch of work home at the end of the day. I felt that I had done a good and exhausting job during the day, and after hours was my time. It's called a life, and I earned it. I felt the exact same way about my students. I made a deal with them. If they worked hard all day doing their best at what was asked of them, they could have a life of their own after school, too. It works. I got the optimum out of each child.

I have also found that *the principle of immediacy* is very real. The sooner the mistake is corrected, the more relevant and effective is the correction. The longer the delay between the correction and the mistake, the more worthless the correction is. If you wait two weeks and then hand a child a corrected paper, you might as well just hand that child a Kleenex. At least that paper would be useful to them. There is also the principle of, "don't pour too much into your glass, because it will spill all over your expensive rug." The brain does not have an infinite capacity of learning and retention per day. Children who do well in school might be motoring along just fine for hour after hour, but the struggling child's glass could start spilling over by third period. Why keep pouring more water into the glass at home? Those Children need to be given a break FROM school so that their glass can empty out, so that they are ready to have it refilled the next day. Struggling children whose retention capacity is smaller and learning rate is slower also need a break AT school, so that their glass is not full up by lunch and every academic endeavor after that is akin to beating the proverbial dead horse. This is another reason why recess, art, drama, music, home economics and industrial arts are VITAL to children's education; they break up the day with a different kind of learning, one in which kids are engaged physically with their mental abilities, and this helps keep everybody from burning out. The children and teachers might actually enjoy school, heaven forbid. This enjoyment spills over into the academic, sit at the desk type of learning because breaks from the desk increase the ability to sit at that desk for long periods and actually retain information. It increases the volume of each child's mental "glass" so that it can hold more information before it spills over, and then they become a behavior problem.

So . . . back to homework. How to make it so that it doesn't create negative experiences in the home? If the teacher gives small doses of penalty-free voluntary homework in the guise of extra credit, there is a chance that a child might benefit, because the work will be seen in a positive light, by both child and parent. This extra credit grade enhancer would be available to the student daily. Reading assignments on a level that are attainable by the child for a half an hour each night seem reasonable. The basic rules are that homework should be doable by the child without much adult help, because if it needs a lot of adult help it should be done in class. It should be of limited duration so as not to adversely impact the child's home life, to which they are entitled, and should be a positive, not negative experience. The beauty of the teacher constantly being in close proximity to the students all day (while they teach and correct as they go), is that it virtually eliminates the need for homework, for both student and teacher. "Free at last!" they shout as they race each other to the parking lot.

Sixth Helpful Classroom Tip: *Make it Real.* I taught at a vocational school for several years and found that teaching students in that setting was light years easier than teaching the exact same students in the high school setting that I had been at before. The students who would only learn how to properly use and manipulate fractions at the high school by the threat of a Taser and the liberal use of mace, were the exact same students who followed me to the vocational school and called out every line of the ruler accurately, rapidly and as joyfully as singing a song. The difference wasn't the fraction, the child, or the teacher; *it was the context in which it was taught.* The carpentry students could relate to the fact that if they cut a solid walnut door 1/8 of an inch too short, they were going to have to take a loan out at the credit union to pay for it or else change their identity, go into a some kind of a witness protection program, and hide for the rest of their lives.

If you want a child to learn, retain, and competently use academic knowledge, it must be real to that child and not just gibberish that some old man is trying to make them learn for no good reason except that they are forced to be sitting in a classroom because their parents are tired of them at the house. "Put the decimal over here because I said so", lacks the power of "Due to the fact that your credit card charges 25% interest annually, by putting the decimal here you will discover that your $500 TV set actually costs you a million dollars." If there is loud screaming and pulling of hair, you can be sure that you have made your point. If the response is "Huh?", "Who cares?" or children catching up on their REM sleep, you have got to re-teach everything. Again and again. Make it real and you won't have to plow the same field so many times. "Well, Sara, I can see on your paper that you injected your pretend patient with one hundred cc's of his heart medicine in a timely manner. The only problem here is that it called for milligrams, and "centi" and "milli" don't mean the same thing. What he's doing on the gurney now is called a "death throe." The teacher now has Sara's rapt attention and can place a pretty good bet that she will learn enough that this doesn't happen in real life.

Real life. What a concept. As a teacher, if you can't find some real, valid reason for a child to learn something and be able to use it in the real world, don't teach it. You are wasting the child's and your time. "My boss threatened to fire me if I don't," is a good reason for the teacher to teach something, but not a good reason for the child to learn it. They won't do it. Translate whatever the powers that be want, which may run the gamut from reasonable to ranting, into something that makes useful sense to the child. This will give the teacher the twin towers of learning: a child's interest, which is motivation to learn, and a practical reason to learn, which guarantees optimum learning speed.

On a moral note, a child's life is valuable. Nobody knows how much time we are allowed on this wonderful planet of ours. The powers that be need to stop wasting a child's precious time just because they can. I don't believe that they have that right. It is up to the teacher to make school interesting if they can. Just make stuff relevant. Making things relevant also helps the teacher on many levels, because it supports the positive atmosphere in the classroom, increases content retention, reduces behavior problems and makes teaching fun. It makes teaching real for the teacher as well as the student.

Relevancy as an optimum teaching tool brings me to another point. Why in the world some school systems are demanding children to perform math such as algebra 12 to get a high school diploma in order to work at the local convenience store, I don't know. High level, very abstract math is usable by a very small per cent of the population and that is what they get paid the big money for. To demand that every child is forced to achieve at this level and punished for it harshly for it if they don't, is just plain bizarre to me. Schools should stop wasting children's time, please. Stop turning children's school experiences into something unpleasant. Make every subject relevant and interesting and those children who find the subject relevant and interesting will excel at it. Those that don't won't. They will excel at something else. Everybody does not need to be or want to be an engineer or chemist. Every child can grow up to be a competent SOMETHING, however. At the micro level, make each lesson interesting and as relevant to the real world as possible. Reading skills are relevant to almost anything, so just make reading pleasurable. On the macro level, there has to be a way where children are allowed to pursue whatever they find really interesting, which will lead to a maximum level of retention and competence. Simultaneously, students should be exposed to many other fields or subjects where they would perform to the best of their abilities. The level of academic attainment and retention might be less, because of less personal interest, but that's alright. They will have been exposed. *Do all of this without punishment. That is how you get the best out of each child.* The world needs great actors, musicians, cooks, carpenters and police officers as well as lawyers, physicists, engineers, mathematicians, and chemists. And behind every last one of these is a great teacher. The classroom should be a place where children can reach their own level of greatness, without the fear of punishment for not being great at everything. It's something to think about. There could be more than one diploma type, certifying different skill sets. This is more to think about.

Seventh Helpful Classroom Tip: *The power of patience.* Except for love, patience is probably the most important quality in a teacher. It is also the quality least recognized or rewarded in the modern classroom as children are pushed to learn more and more at an ever increasing rate. Some school systems are like runaway speeding trains with children clinging helplessly to the side. God help the child who can't hang on and falls off. "Oh, too bad, Julio was such a nice child" isn't a very helpful response to the deceased Julio or his bereaved family. Watching school systems go into hyper-drive has led to me asking myself a lot of crazy questions. When did 1st grade become 5th grade? Did I miss a memo? Should I check my e-mail more often? Who is in charge of the teacher's classroom and why are they acting like they are on methamphetamines? I mean, really. The excuse that some child prodigy in China can perform physics experiments at the age of seven doesn't necessarily mean that little Shonterica sitting in front of me can do the same, or even wants to. She wants to sing. I pity poor Shonterica because she will be punished for her entire life because many school systems have been set up on the model of a rat race. Even better, a Stalinist rat race, where centralized authorities get to dictate how fast the rat is supposed to run. Ignore the child, teacher and parent, because those people are irrelevant. The rat can't run very fast? Fire the teacher, scold the parent, throw the rat out and get a new one. Stalin was not known for his patience.

Patience is a virtue. I have heard that somewhere before. Patience is not only a virtue but is the most important thing that a slow learner needs from his teacher, to become a successful adult. The ability to sit and listen to children read "The grass is real green" over and over until they get it right without shrieking into a pillow so as not to be heard is an ability that most people don't possess. It is also worth its weight in gold. It is the mark of a great teacher. Real patience, the willingness to let a children learn at their own speed, which also means guiding them through a lot of mistakes without making judgments, does not necessarily come naturally to everyone. This is why it is strongly recommended that parents never try to teach their own child to drive. Get somebody else to do it. It will save on blood pressure medication.

All children can learn, but they all have their own pace of learning. It matters not what the teacher does, up to and including holding the child's entire toy collection hostage, it won't, cannot and never will make a child's brain absorb information any faster than it is physically capable of doing. *The art of teaching can be defined as controlling the pacing and matching the learning style for each child in a classroom so that each child is learning at his or her peak efficiency.* If the teacher, who, after all, knows her children best, is not allowed to set up success experiences for the students by matching each child's optimum learning pace and style to content, then the classroom morphs from being a joyful experience into one in which many are bored because the pace is too slow while many others are pressured and stressed because the pace is too fast. *To control the learning pace in the classroom may, in fact, be the teacher's most important job.*

"Pressured and stressed" are two words that should never be in the same sentence as "slow learner" or "struggling child." A child who is not doing well in school will not react positively to pressure and stress. These will derail any learning gains to be made by that child. Patience is what a struggling child needs. And kindness. Keep in mind that "The grass is real green" will eventually be read with fluency and the child will be beaming with pride, because even though this was deadly dull to the teacher, it wasn't the same for the child, whose mind was busy learning something. If learning continues, the small, dull bits become even more interesting to the child and the teacher. Individual reading struggles will eventually be rewarded with an interesting "whole," called a story. It will become apparent to the child that the color of the grass is important to the story, because the crazy troll was trying to hide in it while wearing a neon blue shirt, leading to the downfall that all trolls seem to experience. The only way that a slow learner is going to get to a story is by being allowed to learn the little bits and pieces without being punished. Impatience is a form of punishment because it is showering the child with negative emotions just when he needs positive ones the most. Trust me; a child knows that he is having a hard time reading. He doesn't have to be told. The hard time is a bad enough experience all by itself. Don't compound it by adding more bad experiences to it with any negative emotions, including anger, boredom or impatience. When you are dealing with slow learners, they need not to just learn the material in front of them, but be encouraged in their efforts, because sometimes it is often the encouragement in their lives that is lacking even more than their lack of skills. Many children have been called stupid, laughed at, made fun of and picked on due to their lack of skills. As they get older they will spend more time hiding their lack of skills from their peers and busybody adults than to actually try and increase their skills.

The ability of a teacher to sit patiently and let a struggling child learn at her own optimum pace, which may resemble that of a sleeping snail, will save that child's life. Practice being bored and chirpy at the same time. Start the practice at home when Uncle Carl, the notorious windbag, comes over for dinner. Smile and nod. Not the going to sleep type of nodding, but the pleasurable agreement type of nodding. The smile is important. When a child who is stumbling while they are reading looks up to the teacher for reassurance what she doesn't want to see is Medusa on a bad hair day. So, smile it up, and stay awake. Chew on coffee beans if you have to and tell them it's gum. Bored and chirpy goes something like this: "Yes that IS grass, very good. That's right. Gr is "grrrrr". Let's do the tiger thing. "Grrrr, Grrrrr" Let's see those claws. Come on, that's pitiful. "Grrrr. Grrrr." Good. You're even scaring the lions. Let's go. Wait a minute. Here's another GR. What's that? Green? Now you're cooking with gas. Read that thing. "The grass is real green." You go, girl. I wonder why in the world they are making a big deal about grass being green? Everybody knows that grass is green. What do you mean look at the troll? Well, I'll be dogged; he IS wearing a blue shirt. I guess trolls aren't very bright. I'm not so sure that shirt is blue, however. Prove it to me. Find the word blue in here. Remember. Bl. Bl, Bl, Bl, as in black, bland. What do you mean what is bland? Don't you eat in the cafeteria?" And on and on the teacher and student go, being bored and having a good time with it. And learning. Patience is indeed a virtue. Your children will love you for it.

As a footnote, let me remind you in the middle of this good time that there are fifteen million reasons why a lot of people in some school systems are lined up against you and your slow learners and this patient-learning deal. If you let them, they will not only ruin your good time, but wreck the chance of that slow learner getting a good education, by wrecking HIS good time. Consciously go back to your gigantic view of the importance and power of being a teacher and stay there. You are the shield that protects children from ignorant and sometimes damaging teaching practices foisted upon children from above. Like all shields, your purpose is to take the arrow so that the child doesn't. This is the part of the profession that is not considered a laugh riot. It is also the most important thing that you can do for some children. Children who struggle with academics need their struggles to be as pleasant as possible for them to have any hope of being a successful student. They need to be allowed to learn at their own pace. Come to think of it, a slow Sunday ride enjoying the countryside is usually more pleasurable than a mad dash to the city to see what is going on.

Eighth Helpful Classroom Tip: *Replace anger with disappointment as a positive, behavior changing tool.* If a teacher has had more than a week of classroom experience without getting angry by something that a child has done, they better shake some of their students to make sure that they are not made out of plastic. The virtue of patience is all well and good, but children have a tendency to act like children instead of adults and will occasionally do things that will pop your blood pressure cup. Years ago I was teaching exceptional education at a local high school, when I discovered that I had somehow misplaced my car keys. Children do not have a monopoly on stupidity. I told my students to help me out and keep an eye out for them. An hour later a young man came up to me and said "Mr. Hoatson, Nathan found your keys." I replied "Great! Where are they?" "He threw them on the gym roof." "WHAT?????" It gets even better. When I talked calmly and peacefully to Nathan later in the day (or maybe it was screamed calmly and peacefully, my memory is foggy), I asked him why he would do such a thing. His line of "reasoning" was "I'm sorry, Mr. Hoatson, I found them and didn't know whose they were," implying that he surely wouldn't have done this personally to me, but other than that, flinging valuable lost objects onto a gym roof seems like the sensible thing to do. Again, "WHAT??" Veteran teachers use this phrase a lot.

I was in a first grade class years ago when I saw a little girl reach down to pick up her version of a valuable lost item, a pair of scissors. Brian saw this from across the room. Before she could straighten up and ask who they belonged to, Brian charged her like a lion after a gazelle, hurled her to the ground, put her in three or four professional wrestling holds and triumphantly wrested the scissors free from her death grip. He jumped up and started to go back to his seat, flushed with victory. I went over to see if he had been possessed by demons when I wasn't looking. His excuse for assault and battery was "Well, they were MINE." I see. That makes perfect sense, at least to someone like the Joker who happens to be locked away by the Batman in an *assylum*. Reasoning and children are not synonymous. This is why they are in school, which is to work on this reasoning thing, until they get it down. Until they get into the habit of reasoning and away from the habit of reacting, they can do things that will make the teacher mad, which kicks in the possibility that the teacher may react instead of reason, which happens a lot. The modern teacher is under enormous invisible pressures and those pressures are looking for a release, which can happen when they are made angry. It is human nature. It is also less than helpful, to the teacher or the child. So, the question is, how does one effectively teach when angry, so that the misbehaving child has a chance to learn something from an unpleasant incident? How to deal with a child's misbehavior in such a way as to create a better person? How can a teacher react to avoid damaging a relationship with that child later on down the line? How to preserve the loving atmosphere that has been set up in the classroom all year long? The answers to these questions are the key to creating a safe and effective learning environment. A positive relationship between teacher and student is crucial to optimum learning in a classroom.

Anger vs. Disappointment: Let's look at both of these emotions in the context of trying to make a child do better later on. Which one is more effective? *Anger will push a child away.* Everybody, except maybe Satan, wants to avoid anger and will move as far away from it as possible, either physically or mentally or both. The mind will put up anger deflector shields in the form of flimsy and ridiculous excuses in order to protect itself from attack. Sometimes anger is used as a defense mechanism, because occasionally the best defense is a good offense. Anger may be trotted out to meet anger. There is no real sense in having a nice father and son talk with a truly angry child because NOTHING in the form of reason is going to get through. AFTER the anger subsides, you can get through. So, when blasts of anger are hurled around, no learning of any kind can take place, because everybody involved is in either attack or defense mode. If enough anger is being hurled around it may manifest itself in a physical form such as fight or flight. The flight part is not so bad, but the fight part can get ugly.

Disappointment will pull a child to you. If an adult has established a good relationship with a child, that child will naturally want to please that adult. Use that natural tendency. It is a force of nature, and it is positive. It is an integral part of positive discipline because if an adult is disappointed in a child's behavior it implies a couple of very important things. It implies that the adult cares for the child and fully wants and expects him to be a success in life; otherwise the adult would not be disappointed in a behavior that might threaten a successful future.

Let me get specific here. Let's go back to Brian and his scissors. Instead of just yelling at Brian and punishing, let's throw in an, "I love you, but am disappointed" type of response. "Brian, give me those scissors. I know they're yours. I said give them to me, now. You've got to be kidding me. I thought that you were going to be a veterinarian. What do you mean you are? A good vet makes $80,000 a year. You think they are going to pay you that kind of money to beat up your customers? If somebody borrows a paper clip from you, you are going to beat them over the head with a stapler? What kind of a veterinarian is that? I can see that you are sorry, but that doesn't really do Cheyenne over there any good. You go tell her. Tell her again, you're mumbling. And stop crying, you're not hurt. Now, buck up. There are a lot of sick animals out there that are depending on you to get a good education so that you can help them, not make them sicker. You got me? Now go get a Kleenex and blow your nose. By the way, you're serving Cheyenne her lunch for the rest of the week. And your dessert goes on her tray. You better go get another Kleenex." At the end of all this I have a humble and contrite child who knows that he is loved and will try to do better next time because disappointing Mr. Hoatson hurts deep down inside, because Brian is disappointed in himself. Bingo. That is the best that a teacher can expect from a bad situation. And best is best.

Ninth Helpful Classroom Tip: *Differentiating between "I can't" and "I won't."* The one phrase that is uttered the most in a classroom is, "I can't do this," followed by a plea for help. Due to a couple of laws of science, such as a teacher can only be one place at a time and there are only so many minutes in an hour, it is important to quickly tell if a child really can't do something or if a child really means, "I don't want to do this. I would rather be running wild outside chasing Suzie." It is important to tell what "I can't do this" means, so as not to waste the teacher's time or the child's time due to a wrong response. The teacher should not assume anything. He would be wrong half the time and waste half of the classroom time being wrong. Way too many times the teachers make assumptions due to their own personal views of children. There are teachers who assume that all children are lazy whelps and respond to a request for help accordingly. Their kneejerk responses will be, "Sure you can, you're just not trying hard enough," or "You should be able to do that; we've been working on this for a week. What's the matter with you?" or "Stop bothering me, I'm trying to decipher the latest grading rubric handed down by DOE and I've got a throbbing headache." Now, sometimes that teacher is perfectly correct in his assessment of that child, but there is damage to be done to that child if he is wrong. If a child really needs help and gets the cold shoulder, the following example is what it feels like. I wear glasses because my eyes hover around 320/20 vision. To put it mildly, this is not crystal clear. I am told to read the board from the back of the room. "I can't see the board Ma'am." What I get is, "Don't back talk me, young man. You're not trying hard enough, try harder," or "Stop whining and being lazy. I just don't think that you want to see today," or "We've been trying to see from the back for over a month. You should be able to do this by now." Speaking of crystal clear, this is exactly what children feel they are going through when negativity is poured on their head when they are asking for help for real. After a while, in order to avoid the negativity, they will eventually stop asking for help. In my case, I will pretend that I can see. "How's it going back there, Bill?" "Great. I'm getting every word of it." "I'm proud of you Bill. I knew you could do it if you tried hard enough." Of course, if she had bothered to look at my paper, which she won't until it is too late because she is preoccupied with 10,000 other things, she would have noticed that I had written "Blurr, blurr, blurr" 500 times.

On the other end of the spectrum is the loving "enabler" teacher who will rush over and give way too much "help" to a student. She doesn't even notice that the child left over a half an hour ago and is out back working on his third cigarette because the teacher is doing all the work for him and he doesn't want to disturb her.

What to do when a child says "I can't do this?" My suggestion is go over and see what's up. If a teacher is constantly cruising around the room monitoring children as they are working, encouraging and correcting as they go, then "I can't do this" or

"Could you please help me?" are a natural part of the background noise, because the teacher is in constant "I will help you" mode. If the teacher is in constant help mode, then when she shows up at the "I can't do this" child's desk she will find that there is usually a minor glitch in the child's thinking. The teacher can find and correct it easily by explaining, have the child demonstrate that he understands and can do this on his own, and then move on. The reason that the glitch is almost always minor and easily correctable is that through constant monitoring and explaining' the teacher has never let the child's mind drift out into the deep waters of the Sea of I Don't Get It. The teachers who have the most trouble with a child who says "I can't do this" are the ones that don't check on their children's understanding very often, maybe just on test day, when they become shocked to find out that half the class got a 25% on the test. Shocked, I say! And probably angry about it. Now, I may have been asleep in class, but I missed the "Shocked and Angry Good Practices Teaching Technique" lecture at my college. I bet it was a hoot. The teachers who took this course to heart are the ones who get irritated at being told "I can't do this" by a child, because they don't have a clue as to what their children really can or cannot do. They don't know if the child has a minor glitch in his thinking, doesn't understand foundational concepts or is simply sick of schoolwork. Getting a 25% on a test will tell you what a child CAN'T do, which is not nearly as helpful information as to what the child CAN do. What is their success and understanding level?

The teacher who doesn't monitor a child's understanding level on a regular basis is in danger of that child's mental boat drifting far out to sea into dangerous waters. It will drift into shallow waters, which is "I sort of get this, but I'm a little shaky, can you help me?" into deeper water, such as "I don't know what to do here, I am stuck" on into the ocean of "I don't remember what to do, have been messing this up for a week now and am getting scared that I am going to flunk" into the shark infested waters of "Is the teacher speaking Chinese now? I don't understand a single thing that he is saying and everything I put on paper is wrong. Even my parents are yelling at me, and they're both preachers" until the typhoon takes the boat under, "I hate school." I hate school is not the destination that any teacher wants their children to set sail for. But if the lifeguard is asleep, how is he to know how the child got so far out into the water or even what happened to them. If the body washes up on the beach in the form of a 2% on a test, the rip Van Winkle lifeguard is left scratching his head in wonderment. He will probably be shocked and angry.

The teacher is supposed to set up the school day for each child so that progress comes through a series of progressively harder success experiences. Success breeds success. The flip side of that coin is preventing children from having too many negatively charged failure experiences, especially those that come from challenging backgrounds. Failure breeds failure. Teachers, to create a successful child you have to be a very alert lifeguard. I mean, if the water even approaches the bottom of their bathing suit, go get them and see what's up. "Mr. Hoatson, I can't do this?" "I'll be right there, sweetheart, as soon as I am through with Taronte."

The real question is not telling "I can't" from "I won't." The "I won't" children are easy to spot. If dealt with lovingly and swiftly from an "Oh, yes you will" adult in their life (a little bud nipping if you will), the teacher doesn't have to deal with it often. *The real question is "Where is this "I can't" attitude coming from? Was it from a misunderstanding that can be corrected by a clearer explanation, was it from not quite enough practice for understanding to take root, yet, or is it an organic problem? Is it a biological malfunction somewhere deep in the child's brain?* This is a seriously important question to answer, because some children who answer "I can't" REALLY mean it in the sense of "I don't think that I ever can. I don't think that I can do this now, tomorrow, or in the next century." The truth is that they may be right.

I have taught exceptional education for decades. My play "Mr. Harrison's Classroom: A Documentary" was based on that. I was a basic skills education teacher for adults back when the schools were called mental retardation centers. My second play, "Second Period at the Center" came out of my experiences there. Dyslexia is real. Varying degrees of mental retardation are real. Varying degrees of learning disabilities and brain dysfunctions are real. Anybody can learn. That is not the question. The danger in not recognizing that there is an organic cause behind the child's "I can't" is that the teacher can waste a huge amount of both his time and the child's time trying to force feed skills into a brain that can't accept them. This not only creates a great deal of frustration children by providing them with way too many negative school experiences, further damaging their already damaged self-image, but also takes away the time that could be spent on real learning, which is valuable and pleasant. If a teacher's time is wasted, well, at least they are getting paid. This is not true with a slow learner. Time to learn for slow learners is invaluable and it is precisely this time that is being stolen from them, replacing it with negative experiences. That is a lousy trade for children. I, myself, am a fairly fast learner and learned these principals quickly through my own ignorant mistakes and inexperience. (Again, I pray for forgiveness for my mistakes. I find myself doing that a lot. It helps me sleep better at night. Other teachers find it useful, too.)

Decades ago I was teaching at the mental retardation center, trying to get across money concepts to a group of adults, which are real-world survival skills. There was one man who I will call Bruce who didn't even recognize all of his numbers. He was around 45 years old. I was doing a little one-on-one with Bruce, working on recognizing the number five. Sometimes he would get it and sometimes he wouldn't. As I was merrily sitting there doing what I thought was a perfectly good job, the young but very experienced director of the center pulled me aside and said to me, "Bill, you're new here and are doing great work. We appreciate that. Let me ask you a question. What are you trying to attempt with Bruce, here?" I started explaining that I thought that if he could recognize some numbers that it might be helpful. "Bruce is 45 years old. Don't you think that he has been down this road before?" I began to squirm as the light bulb started to go inside my head. "How long have you been trying this number recognition thing?" she asked me. "Well, about three weeks." The light bulb was getting brighter, illuminating for me my own depth of inexperience. Fortunately the director was a very kind person. "Let us say that after six months you have performed a miracle that 45 years couldn't produce, and Bruce recognizes the number five for the rest of his life. There are a few questions that you have to ask yourself: Why am I doing this, and could those six months of this man's life be better spent? Could he have learned something more useful in those six months?"

I don't know about Bruce, but I learned something invaluable in just those six minutes. Fortunately, those wasted few weeks were happy times for Bruce, because I didn't pile any negative experiences on top of my wasting his time, unlike what happens to slow learners in school a lot. He thought I was funny and didn't even notice that I was committing educational fraud. I didn't either, for that matter, until I got my wake up call.

Years later I was teaching exceptional education teenagers at a vocational school and training them for jobs. Many wanted to be auto mechanics, work on small engines or be carpenters. One week I was in full tilt time table memorization mode and the class was rocking. Everybody, that is, but Jim. He couldn't memorize any of them. We would go over the fours and he would forget them the next day. Mom would go over the fours at night and I would get a blank stare the next day. We would go over the fours in the morning and he would forget them by lunch. I used visuals, auditory and tactile methods, all to everybody's amusement and all futile. I could have done four somersaults into a pool of alligators and it would not have left an impression. That is when I decided to call off the dogs and hand the young man a calculator and show him how to use it properly.

Tool vs. crutch: What is a calculator, or any other learning enhancing device, anyway? Tool or crutch? For people like Bruce or Jim, who are people who cannot perform the skill without the use of the learning aid, the learning aide is a tool. That is why children with learning disabilities need to be identified as quickly as possible, so as to put the proper tools in their hands so that they can succeed as adults. Getting specific with the calculator here, it can be a crutch in the hands of children with perfectly normal brain capacity and cut down on their learning to a level of high competence basic skills. It makes them intellectually lazy. Believe me, when I handed Jim the calculator in my vocational class, it set off a firestorm of protest amongst all the other students who were now eaten up with calculator envy. The wailing and moaning could be heard all the way to the nursing building. They were deeply worried that one of my students was in need of their services. I explained to the class that I was not a greed head when it came to handing out calculators, nor was I somehow mysteriously related to Jim's family. I paved the way for a pathway to EARNING the use of a calculator by their demonstrating to me that they could do the problems correctly and efficiently without one. In that case, the calculator would become a tool in their hands and not become a refuge for the goldbrick. This seemed to mollify the lynch mob and class continued to go on, producing workers that anybody could be proud of.

As a teacher your thinking process when encountering a student who is struggling to do his work is first, "Can't or won't?" Then, if cannot, why not? Keep in mind that mental dysfunctions are invisible to the naked eye. All kids look alike on the outside. That's why, when a bureaucrat peeps his head into a classroom in which the test scores are low, what will go through his head is "Everybody looks fine in here. It must be the teacher's fault.

Escort Mrs. Peacock out to the firing squad, please. And tell her to stop sniveling, it's unprofessional." It would be so much easier if the children were all little Hester Prines and would wear there learning disability on their foreheads for the teacher to see, but it doesn't work that way. Always keep in mind that a child who is struggling mightily at something might have a biological reason for it. "Lazy whelp" is not always the explanation.

Tenth Helpful Classroom Tip: *Make a game out of it.* Whatever it is, from memorizing times tables to knowing all the state capitols, games are perfect for having children learn rote memory skills. This is not rocket science. All children like to have fun. Go with it. Use fun experiences to have children learn necessary, but otherwise boring stuff. They will do it quickly and happily, which is a lot easier on the teacher than pulling teeth from an enraged bull, which demanding dull memorization will devolve into if it just plain, well, dull. When talking about games, what I DON'T mean is the cutthroat, hyper-competitive, I win and everybody else is a loser type of game. Those kind of games are only fun if you're paid millions of dollars, which seems to take the sting out of losing. I am talking about every child having fun. Keep in mind that the bottom 25% of your class, those that are slower learners and struggle at school work, are especially sensitive to being called a loser and will shut down instead of playing the game if there is any chance of having a bad experience. It is precisely these children who will benefit the most from strengthening their rote memorization skills, so it is important that the game is structured to be enjoyable. There are a thousand different ways to set up games and teachers can be as creative as they wish. I will describe one thing I did to help fourth graders learn their times tables.

I am not a big fan of sugar or junk food in general, but especially sugar for children. Children that come from economically depressed backgrounds in particular are notorious for having poor dental hygiene and a school should not use sugar products as a reward for anything. If a reward for doing well in a game is a food product, I suggest that it is as good for the child nutritionally as possible. It can look and taste like a Popsicle, but it needs to be a good Popsicle. This is just an idea that needs to be thought about seriously, because schools could do a lot of nutritional good for children from economically depressed areas, if they wanted too. It is also more expensive to do the right thing which in some parts of the country outweighs doing what's right by children. Such is life in America. In my case, the popsicles that I used were pure-dee junk because that is all the school could afford. I beg forgiveness. The kids liked them and were willing to fight a grizzly bear to get one, which is the exact attitude a teacher wants from students who are trying to memorize their times tables.

I would sit in the cafeteria each day with a class roster for each child. If they thought that they knew their multiplication tables, two through ten, they could come up to me and try to win a Popsicle. All they had to do was get 10 correct answers in a row, my choice of random problems, and they would win their coveted prize. As they answered each one correctly I would hold up a finger in dramatic fashion, so that everybody could see that I was counting to ten. As the child approached ten, the tension would build and those children who were watching this little melodrama would be actively cheering, though quietly, one of their own. Sometimes the kid would blow it, but would come back more determined the next day. This meant that they were actually STUDYING AT HOME OR WITH THEIR PEERS IN CLASS. What a concept. Some studied mightily. Most got their Popsicle.

Then there were some students who wouldn't even come up to try. These are the ones I zeroed in on next. Some wouldn't study at home, in class, with their peers or alone. Nothing. They didn't know jack and were too ashamed or indifferent to admit it. Now comes game two. If they wouldn't study with anybody else they would study with me. I called them one at a time at my table, with the understanding that if they got up to their fives memorized, they would get a Popsicle. I kept track on the roster. The children who had already learned their times tables wanted more popsicles, of course, but wouldn't be able to because they had learned their times tables already. Now comes game three.

Some of the slow learners were having a tough time memorizing the tables, so I turned to the fast learners and told them that the only way that they were going to get another Popsicle was to go coach somebody who hadn't already learned the multiplication facts. If the struggling child succeeded, both coach and coached would get a Popsicle. This set off another round of studying and learning. When a coach thought that her "fighter" was ready to enter the ring, she would bring her to me and we would do the contest. Ten in a row. No mistakes. Sometimes they would do the shoulder message, as if it was the tenth round in a tight boxing match. I loved it. So did they. Now, game four.

Some of the faster learners weren't fast enough for my taste, so I got a deck of twenty random times table cards. If a child could get them in thirty seconds or less, they would get a Popsicle. This set off a frenzy of studying and learning at a higher level. There were students that I figured were probably not going to beat thirty seconds. I still wanted them to increase their time, regardless. I told them that they get could a Popsicle if they could break their previous best time. That was game five. If they weren't increasing their time, I'd throw in another coach, reward both, which became game six. Like I said before, there are some children who have a physiological reason for not being able to catch on, a learning disability of some kind. They would be without a Popsicle at the end of a year, no matter WHICH game they played. I targeted these by building them into the game. They could be timers, or assistant coaches, or scorekeepers, or whatever, just so they were involved and received maximum exposure to the subject matter. They could earn their Popsicle by performing their duties well. This was game seven.

At the end of the day I had gotten the best effort and results from each child that they had to give me. Best is best. The games evolved as I kept trying to get the best from children with a whole range of skill sets. There were no negative experiences outside of occasional mild disappointment, but the peer encouragement papered over any of that quickly. Plus, it was exciting, melodramatic and fun, which is the very definition of being a child. The positive experience of the whole thing has the added advantage of creating a wonderful bond between teacher and student that carries over into anything else that they do together, including the not so exciting reading of the textbook.

This bond is worth its weight in silver dollars, and will pay off handsomely later on with both behavioral control and academic success. So, make a game out of it, no matter what "it" may be. There are entire books written about how children learn best through play, and how play is actually a child's most efficient learning mechanism. It is entirely possible that these authors aren't crazy. They may even be right.

In Conclusion: First of all, may God bless parents, teachers, administrators, counselors, secretaries, janitors, cafeteria workers, coaches, paraprofessionals, mentors, volunteers and any other category of human being that is trying to help raise and educate children. We are all warriors in the fight against poverty, ignorance, illiteracy, crime, violence and hatred and are the human building blocks for an enlightened, just, peaceful and prosperous society for the children who we hold so dear. Education is the beacon of hope for all of humanity, driving back the darkness of mankind's baser instincts and illuminating the pathway to mankind's higher self. There are tyrannical forces in this world that would try to deny the education of its children because educated people will always seek justice and freedom. Anybody who has anything to do with the education of children is paving the way for a better society and a better world. Be proud and fearless in what you do. The children will thank you for it.

It is my hope, that this and all of my writings, have helped somebody, somewhere, do a better job at teaching. I hope by sharing some of my insights and experiences that it may make a child's life better and a teacher's life easier.

Let me share one last little secret. If you, as teacher, can ignore the negative outside forces on you long enough and teach your children, utilizing as many of my sixteen principles of positive teaching as seems reasonable and doable, you will find that those outside forces will be pleased and amazed at your positive results. *They will come to you to ask how you did it instead of coming to you and telling you what to do*, which is often well-intended, but just as often misguided. You will find yourself truly in charge of your classroom and your children. Now, there is a radical thought!

Have faith in children. Have faith that a child working at optimum efficiency in a loving atmosphere is going to get to the finish line. If a child working at optimum efficiency can't reach the finish line, there is something wrong with the finish line. There could be something wrong with the race itself. It has NOTHING to do with the child, who is doing his best, or the teacher, who is humanely facilitating the child to do his best. Stay the course. Always do what is right in the best interest of the child. It will always turn out to be the right thing to do. Learning gains and rising test scores will follow just as sure as the sun rises every day. The children will love being in school and so will the teacher, which is the whole point.

Implementation Instruction Manual

The Miracle Mascot
Behavior Shaping System:

Theories and Practice of Creating
Successful Children and Successful Schools

By Bill Hoatson

TEACHER*PARENT*CHILD*COMMUNITY

PLACE
SCHOOL
MASCOT
HERE

The Miracle Mascot Positive Behavior Shaping System:

Theories and Practice of Creating Successful
Children and Successful Schools.

By Bill Hoatson

Introduction

Before we begin, let me address the style of my so-called writing. I am not a writer, per se. I am a lecturer. I talk a lot. I have had decades of talking in the schools to students, parents and teachers in an attempt to share what I consider valuable ideas on creating successful children. So, what you have here is a long talk, which is different than a book, which is driving my editor crazy, because he thinks that he is dealing with a proper piece of writing. Any and all pretense of real writing and its restricting rules don't apply to a lecture, thank goodness, and let's said editor off the hook. So, let's talk.

Chapter 1

My Background

My name is Bill Hoatson. I love children. All of them. This includes the ones that will drive a tea-totaling teacher to the local bar because of their misbehaviors. Especially those. When a girl walks into a class, mischief pouring out of her eyes, with no intent whatsoever of doing anything scholarly, she being in full tilt entertainment mode, give her to me. That's my girl. I love that girl, buck-wild as she is. Give me the boy who can't even walk down a hallway without getting into trouble. He would argue with his own shadow. That's my boy. I love that boy.

I am able to love the misbehaving child because, over decades of experience with them, I have finally figured out what makes them tick. *Even more important than that, I know what to do to make them successful.* Knowing how to deal with a misbehaving child gives you the power to shape a child's behavior, which allows the adult an emotional avenue to love the child. It is this love for the child that drives the train, because if a child feels that he is loved, he will, willingly or not, allow that adult to shape his behavior. Conversely, if a teacher feels powerless to deal with a child's misbehavior in his/her class, the love glow is replaced by frustration and anger, which emotions will be happily returned, multiplied by three because this, after all, is a misbehaving child.

There is no avenue for positive change in that classroom. The only change may be in the size of the teacher's ulcer, or that the student may eventually de-student himself and drop out of school.

The need for good behavior in a mass setting such as a classroom or a school is obvious, but for some odd reason, there are no real SYSTEMS put in place that actively work towards building good behavior in children. Instead, there are a few punitive systems in place, which are often ineffective in changing the behavior of a child. Out of school suspension does indeed make the classroom easier to control when a child is not disrupting class every five minutes, but sending a child home for an unsupervised vacation is not really going to change his behavior. It may, in fact, reinforce it. A lot of systems are designed to punish and remove, so as to protect the class. This is understandable. It also implies that there is a certain per cent of the children in that school that the school system is willing to write off as incorrigible, and willing to let their lives go by the wayside in the form of crime, poverty, violence, jail, drug abuse, illiteracy, whatever. Anything to protect the majority. This may be a fine attitude for a school system, but it is definitely not fine with me, an individual.

There has got to be a systematic, powerful, easy to use and effective method of positive behavioral shaping in every classroom and in every school to ensure that they educate as efficiently as possible and that all children reach their highest success potential. When I say all children, this includes the one who writes misspelled curse words on the bathroom wall. *The Miracle Mascot Positive Behavior Shaping System is exactly that.* The Miracle Mascot System and this love for all children did not come overnight or easily. I began teaching in 1975. I have taught in economically depressed areas in North Florida and South Georgia for most of my adult life. The more you teach the more you realize the impact the phrase "economically depressed" has on families, thus schools. My students have been predominately African American, with large dollops of white and Hispanic students thrown in. I have taught three year olds in pre-k, kindergarten, 3rd and 4th grade. I have run a behavioral program for out of control 5th graders, and was a behavioral specialist at an elementary school. I have taught exceptional education at the high school level for a decade, trained exceptional education for jobs at a vocational school for years, ran an academy for expelled students, was temporary discipline coordinator for a county for a year, and have run an In-House Suspension Room for a high school. I have spent decades vacillating between being proud of my work and dealing with the same anger and frustration mentioned above which comes from being bogged down in woefully ineffective discipline systems which were allowing children to destroy themselves and ruin the school experience for others. I have been cursed at, broken up more fights than Mohammed Ali, sat in juvenile court with children's school records in my lap and taught in what at times seemed a sea of disrespect. I have learned over time how to get respect and transfer it to students who often don't even respect themselves. I have gotten to feel the love from troubled children, some in prison garb, because I give the love, no matter what they have done. I have found that if you can turn yourself into a beacon of love, a human embodiment of the Statue of Liberty, the struggling and dispossessed will come to you like a moth to a flame, because you stand for the hope for a better future for children and they sense it, no matter how young or old. I have also come to realize that sometimes, depending on the background of the children, a good school or a good teacher is the only hope that they have got. It is because of this that a school must not flinch in the face of the anger, disrespect, frustration and violence that comes from the broken child. These are cries for help that need to be answered, and answered effectively for the sake of the child, the teacher and the school. So, let's set about creating successful children. I present to you 35 years of experience in behavioral shaping in the form of a sheet of paper, The Miracle Mascot.

The bedrock of my belief system is that God has sent you every single child that comes your way, and you have a duty to ALL of them to do your best to ensure that each and every one has a fighting chance at being a success in life. On a more secular level, I have always kept in mind that every student is somebody's child. The parent has probably invested their hopes and dreams and everything else in their child, even those so off the chain that they would disrespect Mother Teresa and then steal her shoes.

As a behavioral specialist I decided early on that sitting and waiting for children to make mistakes and then try to repair them was a huge waste of time and energy, when what really needs to be done is create a school-wide behavioral system that is teacher and student friendly, easy to use and effective. It needs to meet all of the children's needs, from the "A" student all the way to the ones who are flunking and/or acting out and wish that they were ANYPLACE but school. It needs to provide a success path attainable by any child, which will lead them to be as academically productive and behaviorally sound as Mother Nature will let them be. All children are different, which is probably a news flash for the legislature, so the system, in short, needs to allow each child to be all that he or she can be, to borrow a phrase. I have developed a system that can be duplicated anywhere, with ease, and is highly effective in getting the best out of all children, but most especially the bottom 25% academically, and those few percent where most of a school's behavioral problems come from.

It is true that any child can succeed in life if nurtured to live up to his greatest potential. It is also true that any child can easily create enough havoc in a classroom through misbehaving to keep any other child in that class from reaching anything but a maximum frustration point, and ruin the school experience for everybody within earshot, including himself. Unfortunately, that type of child is the one who needs a good education the most, he just doesn't know it or care to, evidently. If you ask any teacher, good behavior is probably THE SINGLE MOST IMPORTANT THING that they could imagine for a well-run classroom, more important even than fixing the lousy pay scale, which tells you something. I am going to lay out a reward system that, when used properly, will pull children towards good behavior. It is to be used for all children, but is specifically targeted to be effective for those children who are really not doing well in school and who cause the most severe school disruptions. There is virtually nothing new in what I say, but decades of experience with struggling children have given me some pretty profound insights into why children act the way to do, and, more importantly, what to do about it. The system, which I call The Miracle Mascot, is remarkably simple. It is the understanding of the insights into child behavior, once digested, that make it stunningly effective. It is a positive, love-based, effort-based and character-based, non-material reward system. To understand how all this works some important ideological underpinnings need to be explored.

The first and most important question that we should ask is, "Why does a child misbehave in school? Why did Jimmy just do that? What in the world was going through his head? Just as the problem of malaria wasn't really tackled until they discovered WHY people were getting infected, (through the mosquito), you can't change a child's behavior until you know WHY he was acting like a stone fool that day. A word to the wise: ALL children will misbehave at one time or another. It is called normal. If you are shocked that children do ridiculous things, then go back to your alma mater and get your money back. Some even have chronic behavior problems that will wreck not only the classroom but their own life as well. I suggest a sense of humor will help tremendously. Seriously.

So, why does a child act up in the classroom? I have been in this business a LONG time, and I can point to two things that drive most misbehavior trains: the child either, in his mind, can't do the work, or the work is so mind-numbingly boring that he rebels at doing the work. Either way the child, being a child after all, will look for fun and entertainment at all costs, which translates into them doing something crazy to make themselves, or preferably everybody, laugh or shriek in terror. The first problem lies squarely on the legislature in their insistence that children are forced to reach some imaginary bar, instead of being allowed to work at their own success level and constantly raise their own bar. The second problem has enough blame to go around for everybody. In short, try and make your class work attainable by the student and interesting, because an engaged student is almost NEVER a behavior problem.

The other source of misbehaviors is a lot tougher nut to crack but one that looms over most troubled children and that is that something has gone wrong in the home or community. If you look hard enough, almost all school problems are home problems brought to school. To understand the power of the Miracle Mascot to do its healing work, we need to look real closely at where these behavioral problems are coming from and the forces at play on children long before they reach the schoolhouse. In short, I have found that in order to help a broken child at school, you need to reach into the home and help a struggling family at the same time. *You cannot solve a child's serious behavior problem in isolation at school.* And spitting them out of school back into the broken home or community to fend for themselves is not just counterproductive, but stupid. If that child is allowed to grow up illiterate, skill-less, frustrated and angry it is not funny for the home or community at large when they become an adult, which they will.

It is hugely important that we have an understanding of what is going on in the homes in modern America to understand what is driving children to act the way that they do at school. I will start with some startling statistics: fully one-fifth of all children in America live in poverty. One half of all American families are merely one paycheck away from plunging into poverty. This economic tightrope puts an enormous stress on the family. The divorce rate has gone through the roof, destabilizing the family unit nationwide. Even worse, most families living in poverty are headed by a single parent who is usually way overstressed and without a support system. What happens inside of homes in economically struggling communities? Often, not much reading takes place, which has far reaching implications for the child later on in school and in life. Mom and dad are being replaced by an abnormal amount of television watching and video games as babysitter. Mom or dad often work at low-paying jobs, leaving them exhausted to actually raise a child, so there is a lot less parental supervision, especially in single parent homes. In economically depressed areas, since there is no real economy, an underground one will spring up in the vacuum, with all of the attending downsides of violence, crime and layers of daily negativity in a child's life. Often times the parents have received no real education. They view the school system with suspicion, but have little parenting skills of their own because of how they themselves were raised, or because they had a child WAY before they were actually ready to in any real sense. Diets are notoriously poor in poverty pockets affecting everything from mom's prenatal care to the child's brain function and mental capacity. Every one of these things and a myriad of others in a struggling home have very real consequences at how a child performs in school, and impacts what he is capable of, even on a good day.

Just to drive this point home, I am going to cite the findings of the largest study of language acquisition in the United States, in a book called "Meaningful Differences in the Everyday

Experiences of Young American Children" by Betty Hart and Todd R. Risely. This study was about children, from birth to three years old, and its implications are profound. By the time a child is three, much of the brain development that the child will rely upon for the rest of his life, is already established. There are doors of learning pathways that are wide open during infancy that slowly close over time. In other words, if you miss certain things at certain stages, they literally cannot be gained back. It is MUCH easier for an infant to learn to speak Chinese than for a sixty year old man. This is because at infancy the brain is hard-wired to absorb language, but that window to the brain does not stay open. It begins closing, making it harder to learn as one gets older. While the sixty year old is straining to learn to say, "Where is my lost luggage?" the two year old sitting next to him on the plane is happily babbling away in fluent Chinese. In Meaningful Differences the importance of early, *preschool* learning experiences was expressed in stark but important terms. Children entering kindergarten are vastly different in their learning capabilities, even at this early age. "What makes the difference?" is the question explored in the language study. The answer holds deep meaning for all parents and educators and POLICY MAKERS, if they would pay attention. The differences in learning capabilities come not from race or culture or religion or gender, but from differences in a family's WEALTH. Period. They studied thousands of upper class, middle class, and poverty families. They found that by the age of three the upper class child had heard hundreds of thousands more words (quantity) and thousands of different words (variety), and most of the verbal interactions were positive (quality). The middle class was somewhere in the middle, and the lower class child had heard hundreds of thousands of fewer words, thousands of words less in variety, with a lot of the verbal interactions being negative. If this isn't a bugle-in-your-ear type of wake up call, I don't know what is. The chart that went with this information is even more revealing, as it is unsettling. Imagine a sideways "v", which would look like this: <, except tilted a little, so that both arms of the "v" show an upward plane for language growth. Even though both the upper class child and the lower class child are both showing language growth for the rest of their lives, the rate of growth is much greater in the upper class child AND THE GROWTH GAP BETWEEN THE TWO CHIDREN CONTINUOUSLY WIDENS THROUGHOUT THEIR LIFE, because their brains have been wired differently between birth and three years old. Now, this is just language acquisition, but it isn't a stretch to imagine that the same type of dynamic takes place in a child in other important fields such as reading and math. Some homes have learning rich environments and some don't. Some have positive environments and some are steeped in negativity. Both have enormous implications for teaching methods in schools, most of which are simply ignored. (It would be interesting to see a plot of where the so-called "F" schools are. I am willing to bet that NOT ONE of them is anchored in a zone where most children come from wealthy families.)

I want to look a little closer at the inner dynamics of a family living under extreme economic stress. The parent or parents are often living in a sea of negativity themselves, see little success in their own lives and are virtually clueless as how to reward a child, much less raise a successful child. Children who are raised in stressed families are often viewed as an emotional and financial burden instead of a little bundle of joy, especially if all the parents hear from the school is how rotten their child is. One of the main attributes of the Miracle Mascot is that it is a flag to rally around for stressed families. *When that positive energy jolt, in the guise of a good effort/ character certificate, hits the household it sets off a chain of positive events, which are immensely important for that child to succeed later on in life. The Miracle Mascot puts an easy to understand positive reward structure into an often unstructured household.* It helps create a positive bond between parent and child and gives them something to be happy about together. It allows an avenue for parents to not just feel pride in their child, but to verbally and physically express it. It opens up an avenue in the child himself to receive love and pride for his hard work, which will internalize inside the child, resulting in positive behavioral changes. *A child with a positive self-image is an entirely different child to teach than one with a negative self-image.* The Miracle Mascot also creates an avenue for positive dialogue between teacher and family and puts the school experience in a positive light. The importance of this cannot be overstated. There is a very good chance that parents in families that are steeped in negativity probably struggled in school themselves and, in non-scientific terms, hated it and everything about it, except maybe the janitor who seemed to be the only one who ever was nice to them or their child. This distrust of school, which leads to avoidance of school if at all possible, is a disaster for the families hovering around the poverty line. The only real way to change the dynamic is for their child to get a good education, which leads to a good job, which can pull the entire family out of the financial ditch that they find themselves in. Unfortunately, what often happens is that a parent's past bad school experiences, coupled with a flow of current negative school experiences in the form of a steady stream of phone calls describing their child as a miscreant, at best, will drive the family away from the only real way to success, which is the schoolhouse! My main advice about saving drowning victims is, *don't wrap the life preserver in barbed wire, snakes and scorpions, because they won't even reach for it, much less grab it.* The Miracle Mascot is a life preserver that will be readily grabbed because it is all positive for everybody involved.

If a child is seriously misbehaving in school, it is because of a series of dynamics between his home life, past and present, and his school experience, past and present. You cannot reroute a child's behavior away from self-destructive to positive unless you can tackle the family-school dynamics as one holistic unit. This is EXACTLY what the Miracle Mascot System was set up for. From my personal point of view, that of a teacher/behavior specialist, I am concerned about not only the smooth functioning of a class or school, in which negative behaviors can seriously derail any positive attempts at real education, but I am deeply concerned for the misbehaving children themselves. If they can't get their negative behaviors under control, they will be lost to us and themselves as positive contributors to society. I am a firm believer that every child has a positive purpose in life, a REASON for being here on this planet Earth, at this particular time. The Miracle Mascot system is one whose aim is to give every child, particularly those coming from stressed or negative backgrounds, a good shot at reaching their full potential. I am going to lay out a few more underlying thoughts that will help you view clearly what the behavioral shaping system is all about, then I will describe precisely what it is and how to use it, at school and at home.

Basic Idea #1: THERE IS NO SUCH THING AS A BAD CHILD. Everything else flows from this point of view, for educator or parent. For real. If you don't believe this I suggest that you do everybody a favor and go home and find a job with inanimate objects, such as auto repair or cabinetry. Teaching is not for everybody. It is the most exacting job in the world, in spite of what anyone thinks, and also the most important job in the world, in spite of the low pay scales. But for you to do any good as an educator there has to be a rock solid belief in the goodness of that child that has been sent to you to take care of. You need to REALLY believe this because children often do outrageously bad, ill-conceived, rude, self-destructive, outwardly destructive, and breathtakingly stupid things, because they are CHILDREN. If you don't believe that there is a worthwhile person under that young lady who just cursed the teacher and slapped her cousin as she fled school campus, then the misbehaviors will simply wear you out and you will quit. The average teacher these days lasts less than five years. OR, you will label a child, such as, "Johnny is the worst child I have ever seen. That boy probably finds a way to be bad in his sleep. PLEASE don't put that boy in my class." Either way, that child, who might have grown up to be a firefighter and save somebody's family from a burning building, is now lost and untethered from any caring adult that may actually get him through the phase of life called, "running amok." Each child was put on this planet for a purpose, and it isn't to grow up to be Darth Vader.

Basic idea #2: THE ADULTS, (meaning teachers, administrators or parents), NEED TO <u>WANT</u> A MISBEHAVING CHILD TO SUCCEED. Everybody knows who the real problem children are in school. To change their behavior you have to ACTIVELY take the time to praise and reward them early and often, when they are actually trying hard and showing good behavior. This takes conscious effort and is what the Miracle Mascot is set up for. I have found as a teacher that the universe will not always send you angels. Trust me on this one. But each child has been sent to you for a reason, which can sometimes at first feel like you are being punished for some unknown Karmic infraction, but in reality a teacher is a lifeguard on the beach of life. Saving societal drowning victims is actually one of your main functions as Teacher, which they probably didn't tell you at college and which legislatures everywhere refuse to acknowledge. Punishment definitely has its place, but you cannot simply punish your way to success. You can, however, reward your way to success. The Miracle Mascot, if used properly, creates a success path for a struggling child.

Basic idea #3: THE CHILDREN THAT NEED YOU THE MOST ARE THE ONES WHO ACT THE WORST.

Basic idea #4: SOME PARENTS NEED HELP IN A BIG WAY. These are the ones who, through atrocious or simply non-existent parenting skills, have unknowingly created a misbehaving Frankenstein Monster that they send lurching into somebody's classroom to wreak havoc every day. They don't need ridicule, scorn or anger, which is often the natural response to them. They NEED HELP. This is one of the functions of the Miracle Mascot.

Chapter 2

Defining the Workings of
the Miracle Mascot.

So, what exactly is a Miracle Mascot? It is a sheet of paper. That's it. Very inexpensive. School systems and parents like that. On the paper will read "This certificate is awarded to" and then leave a blank space for the child's name, then continue with "has done a great job in class for the entire WEEK (WOW), showing both good effort and character. You can be very proud of your son/daughter." Underneath is room for two signatures. Across the top is the school name, and in the middle somewhere is the school mascot. These are simple to make and the cost is virtually nothing. This is obviously not a tangible reward system where children get "things", because a sheet of paper is worthless. The power to change behavior is in what it represents and how it is used. There are actually two Miracle Mascots, for two different sets of problems. One certificate is rewarded WEEKLY for the 90% of the students who have the ability to give a good week, if directed that way. There are a few students, however, that a week might as well be a year, and will never get one, because they are often in trouble by 9:05 a.m. These will be eligible for a DAILY Miracle Mascot, which is a little different system. I will first walk through how the WEEKLY certificate reward system works, then how the DAILY system is different. A lot of what I am going to talk about will be from elementary school experiences, but the same principals apply to older children, but geared towards them at a more mature level.

The Weekly Behavioral Certificate System

Step 1: *Create a "Miracle Mascot" certificate for your school,* using your own similar wording and mascot.

Step 2: *Positive Parental Contact:* At the beginning of the school year the teacher contacts each parent with a really positive phone call, telling them what a wonderful child they have and how blessed the teacher is to have them in their class. (Whether the child's behavior is angelic or more on the demonic side is irrelevant at this point.) Once a positive bond is established between teacher and parent, the cement to that bond is the Miracle Mascot. The parents are informed about how their child can earn a certificate *just by trying hard and behaving well in class* each week. Since these certificates are not based on grades but on simply trying their best to succeed, every child, every week, has a good chance to bring one home and make their parents proud. Each parent is asked to think of a way to reward their child and explain to that child what will happen if they bring home a certificate. This will ensure that each family has their own tailor made reward system. This, by the way, costs the school system NOTHING. It can easily cost the parents nothing, also, depending on what they want to do. The child might get to sit at a special place at the dinner table, or get dessert, or get bike time outdoors, or TV time, or dinner with grandma, or ball throwing with dad, or a trip to the beach, or special pencils, *or whatever crazy thing comes into the parent's mind, because all of it works.* It is just a method of telling the child, "We are proud of you," which is the heady elixir that *really* works to shape good behavior.

The teacher will also talk to the parents about setting up a special place in the house to display their certificates, for all to see. It can be on the refrigerator, bedroom wall, living room wall, wherever. It just needs to be in a *designated special spot.* The power of this cannot be overstated. When you visit the home of a troubled child, after navigating the yard debris, you enter it, and see on the wall, amidst the peeling paint and grime, a few carefully placed good-effort certificates, if you don't find yourself desperately trying to "man-up" and not cry, then you are either legally dead or just a well-dressed rock. If nothing else, the Miracle Mascot Certificate has changed the dynamic in that household from the child being viewed as a burden on the family, to the hope of the family. *The child being viewed in a positive instead of a negative light at home will have important ramifications on how he and his family will view school.*

The quality of the talk to the family about how the Miracle Mascot is used is important. This is especially true for the parents of misbehaving children. One parent of a child who was constantly in trouble at school confessed to me at a meeting that she had made a big mistake. When her son finally brought home a couple of certificates, she basically gave a big yawn and threw them into the trash. His behavior reverted back to whatever disrespectful stuff he was doing before he had *his* efforts totally disrespected. She asked if she could start again and I said, "Of course." This "of course" implies a very distinct and important mindset that is vital for anybody in the world of education. The belief that anybody, whether parent, teacher, or most importantly the child, can be "born again" in a behavioral sense on any given day—that people can create a new, positive, successful self in spite of their not-so-successful past, is the ideological foundation that the Miracle Mascot is built on. The belief that all children are good, including the one that called you old and wrinkly the day before, will carry you a long way. Amnesia and faith are qualities worth cultivating. You don't want any child or parent to be defined by past mistakes. This is a deadly trap that is hard to get out of. One of the functions of the Miracle Mascot is that, for those children with behavioral problems, it is a weekly escape vehicle from a damaged past to a successful future. For all the other students, it is a constant reinforcer that keeps them on the success path.

This bonding of school and parent through the Miracle Mascot takes on increasing importance for those children whose behavioral problems originate in the home and are merely transported to the school. It allows a good educator a portal into a home that may be in need of some sound advice, like a six year old shouldn't necessarily be watching "Friday the Thirteenth" for the thirteenth time or that just maybe dinner should be more than just chips and soda. At the very least spinach flavored chips. I had a child in the first grade who threw spectacular, Fourth of July type of tantrums whenever he got frustrated, which to the teacher seemed like every five minutes. During one of my conversations with him I found out that he had seen every hair raising horror movie ever made. I said, "You're kidding me. Don't you ever watch anything normal, like Shrek?" He looked at me and replied, "Who's Shrek?" You can't make stuff like this up. The point being, that there are a LOT of parents, especially young, single ones, who really need HELP raising their child, because their boat is being swamped by the sea of life, they are ill-equipped to deal with any aspect of their capsizing boat, and if they don't get some help the boat will be lost at sea. The whole family, including the child, will be lost to society in any meaningful way. The Miracle Mascot is a way for the school to bond with parents in a positive way over the successes of their child, which opens the door to "success advice" which may eventually actually be taken to heart. If a teacher works hard at helping a child succeed and has a positive relationship with the child's parent, the teacher slowly becomes viewed as a charter member of the family which gives him a shot at having his parenting advice paid attention to. If a teacher is not viewed as a family member, but as an outsider who is bent on attacking her child, hence the family itself, not only will good advice not be heeded, but for some mysterious reason the phone is never answered when the school calls.

Step 3: *Positive Phone Calls.* The power of a positive phone call: ENORMOUS. The power of a negative phone call: NONE. Worse than none. If the first phone call from the school is a negative one, and it is coming into a household that is not doing so well and is itself filled with negativity, then the teacher will be perceived as just another negative force in their life to be avoided at all costs, thus shutting and locking the door to one of the few avenues of escape from their negative situation, the school house.

Keep in mind that if teachers and administrators are asked to make positive phone calls to children's parents on a regular basis, the ones that aren't already doing so are going to roll their eyes and moan and groan. Ignore it, because it is not their fault. They are so overloaded with idiotic demands from twelve different layers of bureaucracy that ANYTHING that is asked of them at this point, up to and including being asked to put boxes of hundred dollar bills in their car to be used for a spending spree, will be perceived as nothing but extra work. I know this because I have been teaching since 1975. One word from teacher to teacher—Once you have made positive phone calls on a regular basis, you come to realize that, not only is it not a waste of time, but it is the single best thing, besides actual teaching, that you can do with your time. You will find yourself wanting to do it all the time because the experience is so pleasant and positive for everybody involved, that instead of being a chore, it is stunningly uplifting. *The beauty of it is that the more positive phone calls and Miracle Mascot certificates, that you pour into a household, the easier your job becomes at school.* That is what the behavioral system is designed for. I have had parents cry over the phone, literally, when hearing good news about their child, because they had never, ever, had a call from the school praising their child. They thought that I must be mistaken and was gushing over one of the neighbor's kids.

One quick, true story to illustrate this point, and then we'll move on. I was teaching exceptional education at a high school a few decades back, and I had a teenage girl in my class who was in an exceptionally bad mood. She didn't want to do her work, didn't want to be in school, and had it up to here with some man trying to teach her how to write, so she snapped. She began cursing like a sailor during closing time at the bar and then went into full tilt hurricane level defiance mode. My jolly mood evaporated, being replaced with a healthy dose of fed-up, so I picked up the phone to have her mother, who I had never talked with before, come and throw her over shoulder, stuff her into the car and take her home. A pleasant voice answered the phone. The steam coming out of my ears was rapidly filling the room when, phone in hand, I happened to look over at Lucy, who had her hands on her defiant hips, and I don't have any idea what came over me, but I had a moment of epiphany. "Hello, Mrs. Washington, this is Mr. Hoatson from the school. I just wanted to give you a quick call to tell you what a wonderful young lady your daughter Lucy is. She is not only very smart, but if she puts her mind to it she has the potential to be anything that she wishes to be. (Pause) Yes ma'am, she told me that she would like to be a nurse. I'm sure that with hard effort, she will make a good one. (Pause) No ma'am, that's all. Just that you can be proud of your daughter. We'll do our best here to make sure that she gets into a nurses uniform. Have a blessed day." (Click) Lucy was speechless, which was a relief for everybody in the class. But even better, I had Lucy. Even better than that, was that Lucy knew that I had Lucy; that I had unwittingly trapped her in a behavioral box from which there was no escape. "Well, Lucy? How about it? You have a very nice mother who is, in fact, very proud of her daughter right now. How about if we do our work and leave it that way? Or do I need to call back and tell her that I was having one of my hallucinations brought on by stress that teachers have every once in a while, and I really meant to call Sherita's mother?" Lucy, very quietly, sat down and began to do her work. "No, Mr.

Hoatson, that's okay." I went about helping Lucy and the others do their work, and everything was, indeed, okay.

To summarize, Step 3 is to set up a positive link between school and home. The teacher should bond with the parent in a positive way and set up the Miracle Mascot as a common positive goal for their student. The parent and teacher then establish a reinforcing reward system at the house.

Step 4: *Explain the good effort and character certificate system to the child* and tell them how excited their parents are in looking forward to them doing well in school. The teacher will explain how proud she is of the efforts of her students and wants to tell their household how great they are doing every week, so the Miracle Mascot Certificates are a way of doing that. They will also explain how proud the children should feel about themselves when they are trying hard to prepare for their future careers, and that hard effort and good behavior is not only the pathway that will lead them to a successful future, but is what is naturally expected from successful, wonderful students such as those sitting in this very room. After the teacher finishes with her Knute Rockne speech and the deafening applause dies down, go to step 5.

Step 5: *Design a Successful Student Pledge*, which will codify in writing what behaviors the school is actually looking for in a student to award a certificate. "I wish to be a successful adult. In order to do that, I will be a successful student. I will give my best effort each day in class. I will be respectful of my teacher and fellow students and will be treated with respect in return. I will be helpful and kind. I will take pride in my efforts and make my school and parents proud of me. I will succeed." To get a good laugh I would keep reading . . . "And I will give Mr. Hoatson $1,000" and watch them desperately try to find where in the heck *that* is written. Once the school has worded this thing any way they wish, put a mascot on the pledge, fancy it up with a little scrollwork and let it ride. Leave room for three signatures. All the students will sign it in class and the teacher will sign each, and then the Successful Student Pledge will be sent home for the parent's signature and placed in a special spot awaiting the Miracle Mascots that will be forthcoming. A single, larger, class-sized version will be signed by ALL the students and placed on the classroom wall. Now the school, parent and child are welded into a unified success unit.

Step 6: *How to use the Miracle Mascot: The Miracle Mascot is not just an award for good effort, but is a behavior shaping tool to be actively used to bring forth the effort and good behavior that you are looking for from a child.* Teachers and administrators will use the reminder of the importance of the certificate signing every Friday and the reminder of how proud their parents and teacher will be if they keep up the good work. These reminders are used both when a child is doing good work, as praise, and used when a child's behavior or effort is veering way off course, the scientific phrase being, "coming off the chain," to redirect the child back to his success path. Don't let the first thing that a child hears about the certificate that week be, "Have you lost your mind? Now you definitely won't get one and the way you're headed, you may never get one again." Now the teacher has just thrown away any power of the Miracle Mascot to get that child back on track for the rest of the week. And if this was said on Monday morning, it will be a lo-o-o-ng week. *Absolutely do not wait for a struggling child to mess up and then punish him/ her for it, especially if you know that this child has a history of misbehaving.* It may help you, as a teacher, blow off steam, but it does nothing to change the child's negative behavior. On the contrary, it often reinforces the child's own negative self-image, one in which he may very well take great pride in later on in life. In his mind and in his circle of friends, being "bad" can be an honorary term. This is a dangerous mindset for the child if he thinks his main power is to be "bad" and it sinks into his core-into his self-image—and hardens into cement. He will be set up for having a really "bad" life, and possibly a really "bad" and premature death. The last time I checked, it wasn't the role of the teacher to facilitate a child destroying his or her own life. To change a "bad" child's behavior the child needs to repeatedly receive academic success experiences, set up by the teacher (or parent, at home), which is the art of effective teaching, then have him feel the love and pride flowing from the teacher for working hard and being "good." More importantly, this transfers over to receiving love and pride from the child's parents and family for working hard and feeling good More importantly still, is the child receiving the love from the school *and* family united as a single unit with a single purpose, which is to raise a child to be a successful adult. The Miracle Mascot fosters all of the above, if used right. The proper use of the Miracle Mascot is to use it as a praise point as often as needed. If you KNOW that Jimmy is going to do something that disrupts the class by 10:30, which is evidently as long as the boy can last every day before cracking, then start praising him for good work at the crack of dawn. "Will you look at that, Jimmy? That is a great job with your handwriting. Those "E's" are formed perfectly." Five minutes later, "That is a stone cold perfect sentence. Jimmy, when you are a famous writer, I want your autograph. To heck with the autograph, I will come and borrow money. I will stand in line behind your parents." Five minutes later, "You are kidding me. Once we get some of this spelling corrected, this is going to be one cool story. Jimmy, you are a work horse today. I am truly impressed. Wait a minute. (Hold hand up to head). I am seeing a vision. A vision of a young man on stage getting a certificate. I see parents weeping for joy." After the laughter dies down, tell Jimmy that you are proud of him, but don't get the big-head quite yet, it only being Tuesday and all.

The use of the Miracle Mascot is structured to form positive personal relationships between teacher, parent and child. *A positive personal relationship with a child is the most powerful behavior shaping tool of all.* If all of this good stuff is *consistently* happening to Jimmy before his 10:30 crack-up time, it may be just possible that Jimmy can perform well clean up to lunch. Or beyond. Or the week. Or beyond. The truth is, *that most behavior, good or bad, is habitual in a child.* Whether a child responds to somebody opening a door with "Thank you," or "Get out of my way fatso," depends on the habits that a child has picked up in how he responds to situations: polite or rude, peaceful or violent, kind or mean, not cursing or cursing. Breaking bad habits is not easy. Just stand outside the Betty Ford clinic and ask if anybody is having fun yet. It is imperative that a teacher or parent give misbehaving children things that they can do well and then *consistently and systematically praise them for it.* A positive response from that child will become habitual over time, replacing the old, negative and not very productive responses that he/she was used to, such as "Get away from me you old bat, I don't feel like working today."

The idea of consistent and systematic praise is important. The chances are that the girl who declared, "I am going to be good all the time," will be involved in a knock-down, dragged out free-for-all over a certain yellow crayon that she covets a little too much and which also happens not to be hers, is at least 50-50. This is the same dynamic as the person who REALLY means to quit smoking being found out back with Uncle Fred, enveloped in a blue haze, hiding from Aunt Suzie. It is going to happen. Just remember, bumps in the road don't stop a moving vehicle, and if reinforced enough, good habits will replace the bad.

The Miracle Mascot works as a behavior changing tool simply because the feeling of being loved is much more powerful than those negative but also powerful feelings generated by doing "bad" things. The root problem of many poorly behaving children is that they have not gotten much love in their harsh life and so don't really know what it is like to be rewarded for doing good things. They have received way too many negative responses to whatever it is that they were doing, and thus have learned to respond negatively to their life situations. Another way to look at this is to come to the understanding that children from negative home or community environments have simply got to find the school a positive and loving place if there is any hope of shaping their behavior so that they will have positive and product behaviors as an adult. If home is negative and the school experience just piles on negative, then that child is toast. Burnt, crispy, throw in the trash can kind of toast. The shame of it is that the toast in the trash can might well have been the best piece of bread in the loaf, we just won't ever know.

The child needs to feel the external love from teacher and parent for doing positive things, both behavioral and academic. They will eventually feel the internal feelings of love if they get it from the outside enough. It is a natural response that doesn't need to be forced. Once that good feeling that is generated inside by being loved, the child will gravitate towards being loving and kind and will start taking joy from doing positive things. I have had children marching to my office, certificate in hand, declaring things like, "I'm not a bad boy, anymore," "I am a good girl. I am going to be good all the time Mr. Hoatson," or, "I like being good. My dad is proud of me." Now, me not being totally stupid and all, I realize that these are not necessarily permanent statements, but the emotions of children who have had a reputation for doing bad things, when they feel the internal shift of their power source going from negative to positive, borders on elation. And, even if temporary, is real. Seize the moment and build on it. The truth be told, any adult that has a hand in the saving of a child's life, feels the exact same elation. If done systematically, the positive feelings generated by turning children towards a good path in life can lift an entire school to another plane entirely, regardless of the persistent efforts of the legislature the Department of Education to bum everybody out.

Step 7: THE CEREMONY. Making a ceremony out of the presenting of the Miracle Mascot is the school equivalent of the parents making a big deal of their child giving good effort, and adds greatly to the power of the reward certificate itself. So, every Friday becomes Showtime, and the closer to Friday that you get, the easier it is to use the Miracle Mascot as a good-effort/behavior lure because Showtime is exciting. Every Friday every child has a chance to become a star. This is heady stuff for a child. I will describe two models for handing out the certificates, with all kinds of variations possible. First, let me clue you in on something. If you wish to have a lot of power, and I mean Pharaoh type of power, be the one to sign a certificate or make that positive phone call that goes directly into the home and makes mom and dad jubilant for the entire weekend. Zeus and Thor are squeaking mice compared to you and the power that you will amass to yourself. Let me be very specific about this power, because it is like no other. If, in spite of having to be hard on the child sometimes, you are perceived as the constant bearer of good news, both to the child and the family, that constant outpouring of positive energy will make it so a child may actually take to heart what you say to him. He may actually start to do what he is told to the best of his ability. Now THAT is power. The power to positively shape a child's behavior. Come to think of it, it is in a sense a teacher's or administrator's or parent's dream come true. "Looky here, Martha, Steven just did what I asked him to. Without cursing. And he actually did a pretty good job. Quick, call the newspaper and tell them to send the photographer. Call Grandma, too. On second thought, cancel the call to Grandma. She's got a weak heart." On an historical note, never underestimate the power of love and positive energy to make profound change in negative situations. Just ask Jesus

Christ, Martin Luther King, Jr. and Mahatma Ghandi about the use of positive forces to overcome negative ones. It is as real as the force of gravity, so go ahead and amass as much power as you can. It is for a good cause. Plus, you will find that the power to praise is at least fifty times more effective than the power to punish. And what happens when you become the master of this power to praise? You will find yourself quite literally mobbed by kids begging you to tell their parents how good they are doing. I am not kidding. The kids that beg the most are the ones that misbehave the most, because they NEVER get that phone call or certificate and are the ones who are desperately in need of that jolt of love that comes with the certificate. It is a powerful double jolt. The child is praised at school and then runs home and gets to do it all over again. *Use that time when the misbehaving child is asking for a certificate or a positive phone call home. This is what is called a teachable moment, in spades.* "There is nothing more that I would like, right now, than to be able to call your dad to brag about you, but remember, you didn't want to write your story last period. How in the world can I call about that? How about we finish that story and do a good job of it, *and then* we'll give dad a shout, okay?" There is a very good chance that the child may very well actually finish the story, because that child is as highly motivated as he is going to get right when he is asking for teacher to praise him to parent. Frequently use the mention of the praise certificate, which is the portal to a child's positive feedback from the parents. The thought of a child being praised by a parent is an internal booster rocket for that child, which will allow him to get through many rough spots in his school day. Let's get on with gaining positive power. Let's make a ceremony out of it.

PRAISE-CERTIFICATE   CEDREMONY   MODEL   #1:
Teacher, classroom centered. This praise/certificate ceremony
takes place every Friday, in the classroom. The teacher calls up
each child who has earned a certificate that week. As the child
walks forward the class erupts into applause. When she gets to
the teacher, the teacher verbally praises her for her effort and
good character that week and tells her how proud her parents will
be when she gets home. Then the teacher tells her to keep it up.

All children love this. Some will get certificates every week.
That is how they are built internally-for success. The Miracle
Mascot is reinforcing a well-built structure to last into adulthood.
Not all children are like Juanita, who will have her entire
bedroom wallpapered with Miracle Mascots by Thanksgiving.
Some children don't have a positive self-image; don't have the
same internal success structure as Juanita to fall back on. If
they do have an internal structure, it is one of expecting to do
badly, to fail. With this child, you are going to have to build the
internal success structure itself and have it replace the failure
structure that is already there. When a child who rarely gets a
certificate approaches your desk through a sea of applause, then
it is REALLY Showtime. "Well, Mr. Washington, I am deeply
impressed with you this week, yes I am. You might just earn
that police officer's uniform yet. As a matter of fact, let's call
mom now and tell her. I've got time for three phone calls today
and you, young man, will be the first. Don't worry; we'll break
it to her slowly. We don't want her to faint at work. (The class
cracks up. The boy beams with pride.) "Ms. Washington, this is
Mr. Hoatson at the school. You will never guess who is standing
in front of me with a certificate in his hand. I'll give you a hint.

He was the hardest working boy in the class all week. That's a pretty good guess, but let's make sure. This boy here is about four feet tall, blue shirt, Mohawk haircut, yep, that's him alright. Why don't you talk to him for a second and tell him how proud you are. Here you are Robert, it's your REALLY happy mother. Good job."

A few words on the certificate/phone call combo. I purposely make the positive phone calls in broad daylight for all to see and hear. Having other children see how cool it is to be talking to a happy mom or dad is worth its weight in gold as far as behavior motivation goes. There is not a child on this planet that doesn't want what Robert just got—an outpouring of love from his teacher and parent, right in front of his peers. It doesn't get any better than that for a child. The ceremony of the Miracle Mascot makes this type of interaction part of the system and it becomes part of the day. These Fridays create a wonderfully positive atmosphere for a school and for children. I usually make my phone calls in groups of three's, with a mix going towards both the always well-behaved child (success reinforcing) and toward the newly well behaved child, for at least this week, anyway (success building), so that nobody feels singled out or labeled. I also always make the positive phone call in conjunction with the Miracle Mascot when a notoriously misbehaving child earns her first or second certificate because *it will get the parent pumped so that something special happens at that house when the child presents the Miracle Mascot to mom or dad.* What you DON'T want is for those first certificates to be met with "So what? Go mow the lawn." If that happens, you not only don't have a behavior shaping program in that child's head, you now have one hacked-off child to deal with on Monday whose view of your certificate leans more towards toilet paper than an honorary sheet of paper. This is why the early bond is established between teacher and parent, so that they are on the same page. Many parents of misbehaving children don't actually really know how or when to reward the child properly to get better results. The Miracle Mascot puts shape and form to a very real way to reward their child. Once the parent, by following the school's lead, feels the love and pride that goes back and forth between parent and child when a certificate is presented and acknowledged PROPERLY at the house, the family dynamic has changed with a pathway for positive energy to flow, a pathway that may not have existed before. *This is huge for the future of deeply struggling families.* In other words, once the love is felt, the teacher doesn't have to explain anything anymore. And once the certificate ceremonies have taken place for a while and actually become part of the school's daily routine, you don't have to explain anything to anyone anymore, because the whole community knows about it and is excited.

Phase two of the classroom ceremony is the visit by anybody from the principal to the guidance counselor to put in their two cents worth, which is way cool for the child. There should be at least two places for signatures on the praise certificate, so that when the principal comes in she can ooh an aah over the children who have gotten a Miracle Mascot and sign each one. This allows the administrators to add their weight to the teacher's classroom control, as well as consolidating all the power that accrues from the power to praise. It also helps administrators keep tabs on the troubled children in the school in a very positive way. If one of the troubled children earns a Miracle Mascot, and the administrator is feeling real sporty, she can throw a couple of Lion King stickers on the certificate for good measure and call Mom, to boot. The more fun that a child has at one of the ceremonies, the more powerful the draw towards good behavior there is, so live it up!

The record keeping on this is teacher friendly, as ALL paperwork should be. The teacher makes a copy of his class roster and simply records the date every time a child gets a Miracle Mascot. Not only is the teacher keeping a success record for each child, but it allows the teacher to see children's success patterns early on, which will allow them and administrators to zero in on those who need special attention.

PRAISE-CERTIFICATE CEREMONY MODEL #2: Administrator centered, in the lunchroom. An administrator (counselor, behavior specialist, vice-principal or principal,) will sit up on stage or in a highly visible setting in the lunchroom where children can see others come to get their certificates signed. A table will be set up for the administrator to be at with a seat next to him for each child to sit, while the praise certificate is filled out and signed. The table should be bedecked with copies of the school's Miracle Mascot and a banner with the wording "Great Week." Behind the table should be 20 or so chairs, where children are to be seated to await their turn for their "moment in the sun." The power of the praise certificate still lies in the hands of the teachers, because they are the only ones who can send a child to the stage to receive one. The paperwork for the teacher is zero. The administrator will have a class roster for each class, and will simply record the date next to each child's name as they receive their certificate. The advantage of a mass setting over a classroom setting is that the "Showtime" is bigger and fancier and a child gets to sit in a place of honor while he waits patiently for his signing and words of encouragement from the administrator. While the child is sitting, he gets to bask in the glow of accomplishment in front of a large portion of the school instead of just his classmates. This "basking in the glow" thing is worth a lot for children whose attention from the school or classmates is frequently negative. The dose of positive attention that they are getting is a very powerful motivating force to try hard to do well, because the attention is coming from administration, teachers and the child's peers, all at once. As a child looks out over a sea of faces looking back, waving and smiling, and the principal is telling them how proud she is of him, what is going through the child's head during the next week is, "Boy, I wish I could do that again," and they will strive to do so. The more enjoyable, hence memorable, the praise certificate ceremony is, the more power to shape behavior flows to the giver of the certificates: teachers and administrators. There can be a special seat on the stage for the teacher of the children getting the Miracle Mascots, so that teachers and administrators are signing together. A really good part of the mass ceremony is that administrators can get a real feel for the pulse of each student as the year goes by, a feel that is hard to get from an isolated setting such as an office. Another plus is that it puts a very positive spin on what the administration and school is all about. Often times the only time a child sees an administrator is when that child is in trouble. Administration can sometimes be seen in a negative light by both the misbehaving child AND the exasperated parent, who is often exasperated at the wrong person, it seems. Positive attention given to a previously misbehaving child puts an entirely different face on the school from the parent and child's point of view and will pay off in a gold mine of goodwill in the future. If a child is going to get a Miracle Mascot, the parent can even be invited to lunch to applaud along with everybody else. Get grandma out there, too. The more the merrier.

PRAISE CERTIFICATE CEREMONY, PHASE 3: INTO THE COMMUNITY. So far, I have detailed how the Miracle Mascot can wed the classroom and the outlying family into one cohesive success unit for the child. To push the Miracle Mascot to an even higher level of effectiveness to create hard working, responsible young adults that the entire community can be proud of, you simply expand the scope of the Miracle Mascot to include the entire community. If this is done, the rewards for the school system and the children in it will be astounding. The business community can get involved by placing a Miracle Mascot in the window, which signifies that they are part of the reward system. *The business community will get on board BIG TIME because it is in their best interest to have the school system to function at a high level of success to produce a skilled and educated work force as well as productive citizens, also called good customers.* Not only that, it is just plain fun to reward children for doing good. So, business community, have fun and attract customers at the same time. This does not have to cost anybody anything, just be creative. When a child enters a store, Miracle Mascot in hand, just make sure that something special happens to that child. It can be anything from the child getting to ring a "success bell" that is set up for that very purpose, to getting a special pencil, to the family getting a 10% discount on an oil change. Briefly, discounts for the parents on something for their child's hard work at school REALLY pours positive energy into the entire family *and* business. The child can receive something from the business, like a key chain, with the stores logo on it for virtually free advertising. The child can receive a personal handshake from the managers and be toted around the store on their back horsey style. *It makes no difference whatsoever what the business does, so long as it does something positive to acknowledge the accomplishments of that child*, instilling self-pride, family pride, school pride and community pride into that child, which if done enough will last a lifetime. Heck, a family member of the business can make homemade cookies and hand them out. Other organized sections of the community that could recognize and reinforce the Miracle Mascot are places of worship. Any place of worship, any religion. This costs nothing, but can be a very powerful good effort/character reinforcer if the congregation acknowledges the children who have received praise certificates that week with a round of applause as they stand in front of the adults. This is powerful stuff. The Miracle Mascot System is designed to weld entire communities into a single, unifying force to create and reward successful children. It creates a universal language that can be shared in any setting. When an administrator, or parent, or business person, or cleric, or friendly neighbor asks, "Did you get an Eagle, Panther, Bulldog, or Lion today?" (Whatever mascot that applies), it means the same thing to everybody, which is "Did you do a good job this week?" It also has an important subliminal effect on children, because it implies that they are expected to try hard to do their best at school. There is no excuse, really, not to get a Miracle Mascot weekly, because what it is asking is doable for every child, simply try their best and behave well. The community wide high expectations for their children's effort and behavior, being subliminal and all, will over time have a very positive effect on all of the children in that community and the children don't even know it. The adults do however, so they will just keep consistently rewarding good behavior, reinforcing the school.

Basic Idea #5: *The Power of Rewarding EFFORT.* As far as academics are concerned, the Miracle Mascot rewards effort, and nothing else. A child could be flunking and get one. As a matter of fact, *it is very important that poorly performing students get credit for their efforts,* because if their only reward is to struggle for nine weeks and then be slapped in the face with an "F" they will soon give up and go do something that is a lot less humiliating and more rewarding, such as robbing the local convenience store or making $500 an hour selling drugs. *Even prison is less humiliating than failing daily in front of your peers at school. Let that sink in for a minute.* For a long time now there has been near constant tinkering on schools by people who don't really know what they are doing, creating policies that may sound good, but the reality of which impacts negatively on many children in school. Just constantly raising the bar on children as a policy means that a lot of children are forced to spend much of their waking hours struggling to please somebody, somewhere, floundering at things that they are not yet intellectually capable of doing as opposed to being allowed to work and stretch at their own success level. Working and stretching at their own success level is the very definition of optimum learning, with the child happily raising his own bar every day. *Just as success* *breeds success, failure can become habitual, also. A teacher or parent doesn't want a child to be exposed to too many negative experiences at school.* The damage can be lasting, just as a series of positive experiences are lasting. The bottom line is that if a child isn't rewarded for his real efforts in school, regardless of academic grade outcomes, the struggling child will eventually give up his intellectual efforts and go into entertainment mode, which, in educational language, is called a "behavior problem." Thus, even though the Miracle Mascot works well in all schools, it is especially helpful in rigid schools where slower learners aren't really allowed to work at their own speed and receive a steady dose of negative experiences as they fall farther and farther behind. The Miracle Mascot puts an effort based reward system at the teacher's disposal, filling what would otherwise be a vacuum. All that can be reasonably asked of a child is to do their best. If the teacher gets the best out of a child, well best is best.

A few more words on *effort.* Studies have increasingly shown that it is much more effective to praise effort in creating a successful child than to praise intellectual ability. If you tell Darlene, who gets As in class, how smart she is, you are also sending a message to without knowing it, to Suzie, who gets D's and F's, that obviously the reason that Darlene gets A's and B's is that she is imbued with "smartness," which is obviously lacking in Suzie, (from her point of view) so, in Suzie's mind, "Why bother? Why try hard because I am not smart? I even have physical proof: D's and F's on my report card. Boy, I sure wish I was smart like Darlene, but I'm not, so instead of schoolwork I think I'll get stoned and watch six hours of "Teletubbies," instead." This is the exact thinking, with many variations, that goes on in the minds of struggling students everywhere, and is exactly the opposite of what a teacher really wants to convey. The teacher needs all children, especially those that struggle, to believe that the real key to success is consistent effort coupled with the ability to never give up. You want the children not to be afraid to make a mistake, but to view it as a learning experience instead of as a sign of failure. "I am a success," or "I am a failure" becomes an internalized self-view. The Miracle Mascot is a success antidote to those children who are being constantly battered by subtle and not so subtle messages that they are failures. "Success Breeds Success" should be emblazoned on every school wall. This simple but true axiom has profound implications for the way that we run our schools and interact with our children. *The Miracle Mascot gives the chance to systematically reward good effort, which is the building block to success. Do not focus on test scores or other distractions. Focus on getting the best effort out of all children, by going to their individual success levels and reward their efforts to go beyond. The rising test scores will follow.*

Basic idea #6: *Because of their negative backgrounds, some children don't believe in the concept that people are basically good.* They will, in fact, think that you are crazy for thinking so. This little gem of an insight has deep implications for some of the children at your school. Some children already live in the land of goodness. For these children the Miracle Mascot is simply a reinforcer so that this behavior lasts through adulthood. Some children have heard of the land of goodness, but, due to their negative experiences with life, such as deprivation, violence and harshness, it is a long, arduous journey to get there. For these children the Miracle Mascot is a tangible guide through the swamp of negativity for both child and family to get there. And then some children, for whom life has been too hard, don't believe that a land of goodness even exists, so they are not going to suit up for the journey.

True Story: I was teaching at a high school, listening to the kids discuss who shot who at the "club" over the weekend, when I decided to tell them about my weekend. I told them that I went to a very large "club" often, in major cities where 250-350 people meet on the dance floor for three days of contra dancing, which is square dancing on steroids. The atmosphere there is always pleasant, loving, and fun. I told the students that I could leave my entire wallet, Id's, credit cards, money and all, on a table in the room on Friday and pick it up totally intact on Sunday and drive home. After the howling of laughter died away and the admonishments to not drink before class stopped, a serious discussion followed, which can be summed up in one word: DISBELIEF. This is the same howling of laughter and disbelief that greeted an announcement over the intercom for somebody to please turn in a purse that was lost. The same laughter and disbelief when told that a child got an "A" on her test because of hard work and studying, instead of cheating. *This laughter and disbelief in the fact that people actually do good things is not just an outside view of others, but a direct reflection of the child's own self-image.* A school has to deal with this destructive self-view, because a child's self-image is responsible for how he will act in almost any situation, including the classroom. To some children the land of goodness is at best a complete fantasy or at worst a cruel hoax. These children will be doomed to a life of negativity, arguing, complaining, disrespect, violence, hate and danger, because this is their norm in their own life experiences. It becomes the norm in their own head, which is where everybody lives. If both the family unit and surrounding community are steeped in negativity the only real way out of the box is for an organized structure, such as places of worship, Boys and Girls Clubs, sports groups, or in my case, HUMANE SCHOOLS, where children can actually see glimpses of the land of goodness and then feel what it is like to live there. The Miracle Mascot is a system that, once set in place, gives children the chance to experience the fruits of what it is like to try hard and be good until it is internalized and becomes a living, breathing part of them. All it takes is the willingness of adults to consciously reward children for good effort and behavior, sometimes frequently, instead of simply punishing bad behavior. The land of goodness needs to be in the mind of the adult as the destination for *every child,* no matter what crazy stuff the child is doing at the time; then it is just a matter of finding the right map to guide the child out of the woods. The Miracle Mascot, if used with effectiveness, purpose and belief in creating the "good child," is a very good map. It is also the antidote for exasperated teachers who unwittingly blurt out less than helpful statements like, "You can't do anything with that boy. He's bad", and other similar self-fulfilling prophesies.

Basic idea #7: A "bad" child loves being labeled "bad." If your first reaction is, "Huh? What's up with that?," then let me tell you another true story. I had a profound moment a while back, which, if you are paying attention to children, seems to happen quite often. On this day I was paying a LOT of attention to a first grader who had a history of being perpetually in trouble, but who had recently, with tremendous effort, earned himself a few Miracle Mascots. Three weeks in a row. I was escorting this first grader down to my office to try to find his mind, which evidently he had lost back in the classroom during his spectacular tantrum. His footsteps went from walking to stamping, when it came rolling out: "I am sick and tired of being good." And he meant it. I had to turn away from him so that he wouldn't see me laughing. Ah, the terrible burden of being labeled good. Being expected to be good. All of the time. What a crushing burden this can be.

The dynamic of the Miracle Mascot to shape the behavior of a child away from the dark side and towards becoming a more positive, productive human being is essential when seen in the light of how a bad behaving child feels about himself. Being bad is a shield against the overwhelming demands of the outside world. If you are labeled "bad," life becomes easy, in a twisted sense, because absolutely nothing is expected of you. Schoolwork too hard? Just act like a jerk and get thrown out of class. Is the entire school experience too painful? Simple, just act like a bigger jerk and get thrown out of school. The ex-student is happy because he gets to hang out with other unsupervised kids and live the pirate life, which consists of looting and pillaging. The teacher is happy because now she doesn't have to babysit Baby Face Nelson anymore. The only problem is, the child's life is effectively, in any kind of civilized sense, over. Now, it is perfectly understandable for the child not to see this, but the adults standing around him better have a clearer view of the situation than, "I don't care if he drops dead. At least I'll get a little peace and quiet around here." The jails are full of semi-literate, angry young people with the negative self-view of "being bad." Every one of these young people used to be somebody's small child with a bright future to contribute to society. In my humble opinion, no child was put here on earth to live a life of violence and fear, locked in a cage. That, to me, is the bottom line. *For children who live in negative environments, school is WAY MORE than a place to go and be taught academics.* In every school there needs to be an organized, systematic way of creating positive, helpful, intellectually sound, hard-working children with good character. The Miracle Mascot System is just such an organizing tool. For some children the praise certificate is a sheet of paper symbolizing all that is good about being a student. For other children and their families it is much more than a sheet of paper. It is, quite literally, a life preserver.

Step #8: The DAILY Miracle Mascot. Everything that has been talked about so far has been centered around a very effective weekly reward system that will, over time, help at least 95% of the children in any school become more successful. What about the few children in each school that are so damaged or dysfunctional, for whatever reason, that they can't last a day, much less a week? If they go for two hours without turning the classroom upside down, you will notice the teacher in the corner of the room, on his knees, tears flowing down his face, as he is thanking God for this miracle. Every school has a few children like this, and it is imperative that a system be in place to help the chronically misbehaving child, not just for the child's sake, but replacing teachers every other week gets expensive. This is not even touching upon the damage done to the other children who are exposed to a very unfunny three ring circus every day, instead of being educated at what was supposed to have been a school. I'm not sure how old the phrase "one rotten apple can spoil the whole barrel" is, but it is one of the truest pieces of wisdom around. If the teacher is helpless to get Frederick under control, don't be surprised to find Billy, who used to be polite, kind and helpful, off to the side kicking cowering little Jimmy just for the fun of it, all the while chain smoking cigarettes. The moral of the story being that an out of control child in the classroom is poison.

How to help the uncontrollable child control himself, which will lead to a successful child, which will lead to the teacher actually enjoying her teaching experience? First, identify the children who won't respond to the weekly Miracle Mascot, because a week to them is like a year to a normal child. It would be like the teacher being told in September that he is doing an outstanding job and he will be paid handsomely for it in June. What? Among other things, I am wondering how outstanding of a job he will be doing in October. Use the weekly Miracle Mascot as a sieve, because after a while all that is left are the few that have proven themselves incapable at this time, to earn one. It is this child that is in need of success experiences and praise the most so as to correct his behavior, but he is the one getting the least praise of anybody, unless you regard cursing as being positive. Once the chronically misbehaving child has been identified, they are put on a DAILY Miracle Mascot Reward System. All of the rules apply as to the weekly, but it is much more structured. A Miracle Mascot is taped to this child's desk DAILY. The certificate even says DAY on it instead of WEEK, and a long conversation has been had with the parent about the importance of asking for, and reinforcing the Miracle Mascot on a daily basis. The DAILY certificate is different than the weekly one because it has five circles on it somewhere, which will be a place to put a cool sticker on it every hour or so, if the child is trying hard and behaving himself. If the child earns five stickers that day, then the certificate is signed by the teacher and the beaming child is paraded down to the principal's office to receive the principal's special sticker, signature, and hug. After that the child takes the certificate home to mom, who goes nuts and celebrates in a predetermined way. The now proud child returns to class the next day and, hopefully, will earn another one and then another, *until after a while he doesn't need the daily one anymore*, and loses his training wheels to join all the other children in their weekly quest for the weekly dose of positive energy because now he can actually wait that long. VERY FEW children will need the daily reward for a long period of time. Among other things, I have taught exceptional education children for decades and will tell you that there is a slight percentage of children who are so emotionally disturbed that they will absolutely not respond to almost anything that you can do in a normal classroom setting, because it is too much for them to handle. Those children that do not respond to a well-executed daily praise reward system should be looked at carefully and are candidates for a smaller, more controlled setting run by highly qualified people so that they can get the proper help to be successful. For the other 99.9% of the children in a school, the Miracle Mascot will take care of business.

It is important to actively work on making the daily Miracle Mascot succeed, because it targets the most disruptive children.

Here are a few daily reward rules to be a success. I know that I have said most of this earlier, but I am going to get very specific here.

A). REWARD EARLY in the day when the child does something good. The first ten minutes of class will do just fine. Give a sticker and specific praise, such as "Jimmy, you started your assignment on time, just as I asked. Good job." Rewarding early in the morning sets a positive tone for the entire day. There are five sticker slots to fill, so the first few can come early. The child will have to stretch some to get the last couple. Once they have three or four, you've got them right where you want them. "Have a seat Jimmy. Remember, only one more sticker and you get to have your picture taken with the principal. Yes, he'll let you wear the special football helmet that he has in his office." At the beginning, the teacher may even want to call mom in front of Jimmy. "Yes Ma'am. He actually has three stickers and you can be proud of him. I think that if he keeps this up, you better get your party shoes on. Sure, you can talk to him." Children who have never felt success have got to feel what it is like. Once they feel it, the rewards of succeeding become self-generating. Once it becomes self-generating the teacher and parent have to do less and less. That's the beauty of it. If rewarded EARLY and OFTEN at the beginning of the year, by the end of the year everybody's life becomes much easier, as the child finds more and more success experiences at school.

B). REWARD EARLY, part 2: This time I mean age. The earlier in age that you can correct behavioral problems, the better. It is also easier. What you don't want to do is wait until a child is sixteen and put a sticker on his Miracle Mascot because he didn't rob the lunchroom that day. Stickers don't work so well with teenagers. Tattoos, maybe. If a child is a serious behavior problem when they are 15 or 16, you actually have a bona fide serious problem. The main problem is that their behaviors have become so ingrained in them, as well as their negative self-view, that it is probably easier to cure somebody from a deadly narcotic addiction than to change the way an older teenager behaves. Bad habits are hard to break. It is much better to identify behavior problems EARLY in a child's life, when you can use something like the Miracle Mascot System to not just expunge bad behavioral habits but to replace them with success habits, which will last the child into adulthood. Any educator has had that moment when they are watching a small child doing something REALLY wrong, like stealing from the teacher's purse and then bragging about it level of wrong, and find themselves thinking, "That boy isn't going to make it to adulthood. They will either be in jail, or dead. Come to think about it, they will be lucky to make it to twelve." Well, there is nothing wrong with the thought process. If you watch, you can probably fairly accurately predict which children are trouble-bound. It is the response attitude of the adult that is important. If it is "Tsk, tsk, tsk, what a waste" the adult can probably expect visits to the local prison later, to check and see if the grown version of this child needs any new reading material. That is nice and thoughtful and all, but didn't help the child in the least. The adult that is actually a help, instead of an innocent bystander at a train wreck, is the one whose thought process goes more like this: "Boy, Johnny is ruining himself. I love that boy and will absolutely not just stand around and watch him destroy himself. Let's take care of business right now." This is the type of attitude that is behind the Miracle Mascot and what makes it work.

C). ALL CHILDREN SHOULD BE TAUGHT AT THEIR SUCCESS LEVEL, and then stretch, *but it is imperative that the chronically misbehaving child be given work that she can actually do,* because their frustration level is very low. Twenty thousand leagues under the sea type of low. They get frustrated easily, act out, get yelled at, act out again in a more Shakespearian manner, then get removed from class. Their day has no success flow whatsoever, constantly being interrupted by their own inability to work for any length of time. This is bad enough, but when Mt. Vesuvius goes off, spewing ash everywhere, it takes out the entire outlying village with it. There will be no success flow in a class if there is no success flow in a misbehaving student. That child has GOT to be working at their success level, I don't care what any bureaucrat or politician says. They can say anything they want, because they are not in the classroom. If a fourteen year old boy is reading on a second grade level, the teacher has two choices: **Either** teach him at that level, keep praising him for a job well done, keep making the reading incrementally harder and praise him for continuing success, and eventually watch the boy happily rise to the third grade level, then fourth grade level, etc. He will eventually rise to the highest reading level his brain will allow him to obtain, because that is what brains naturally; automatically do if the tasks are pleasant. **OR**, the teacher can desperately try to jam 8th grade material down the boys throat because somebody has predetermined what is right for this boy and is going to tie this predetermination to the teacher's paycheck AND the school's funding. This frustrates the boy AND the teacher, and sets off another round of the boy constantly trying to entertain himself in inappropriate ways, because that is a whole lot more fun than being tortured on a daily basis. The teacher, in the meantime is checking out the glories of working in the wonderful private sector which she has heard so much about, taking her invaluable teaching experience with her. Teach that misbehaving child at his success level, praise a lot, let the child enjoy his school experience, and low and behold, the misbehaving child has disappeared through a trap door, replaced by a young man who is actually pleasant and fun to be around.

I am going to take this fun to be around thing a little further. It is virtually impossible for the teacher or anybody else in the room to have fun or enjoyment if the teacher is always in cranky discipline mode because of a chronically misbehaving child. I don't know how to break this to the test-driven powers that be, but the link between enjoyment and learning and unpleasantness and not learning is very, very strong. If children were taught at their success level and then stretched, most of the teacher's behavior problems would simply evaporate. So, why isn't this automatically done? Having been a teacher for decades let me shed some light on this. First of all, there are a lot of children sitting in front of you and they are on several different success levels, some far behind, some way ahead. Teaching a bunch of children by yourself and making sure that each child is not frustrated by work being too hard, or bored because work is too easy, is not just tricky business, but nigh on impossible. It is less than helpful that some school policies actively discourage the teacher from going back to a more comfortable learning level for a child, and insist that the best way to get a child on grade level is to force him there, and punish him if he doesn't get there. This is absolutely backwards and creates a lot of totally unnecessary and counterproductive behavior problems. Some people at various state levels are beginning to understand this dynamic and are now talking about what is called "curriculum differentiation" in each classroom, meaning to have children work on suitable levels in each class. The only problem is, they don't seem to want to fund this properly, and just expect teachers to do this by themselves. I am all for curriculum differentiation. Put a teacher's aide in every elementary school classroom in America, so that the teacher can teach the bulk of the class and direct the aide on how to give the small groups the one on one attention needed by those off of grade level, both above and below. School systems in the long run would save money, because most of their behavioral problems would disappear or at least become more manageable and all of the vast amount of money that is spent on dealing with behavioral problems could be spent on positive, successful things, like the aforementioned teacher's aide. If you couple letting children learn at their success level with the Miracle Mascot effort/character based reward system, the success of each child is almost virtually guaranteed.

D). The paperwork on the daily Miracle is also very teacher friendly. Simply make an individual chart for the child and record how many stickers the child earned each day. It's that simple. The child may be floundering and get just a few, until the success habits kick in, or he may take like a duck to water once the praise hits both at school and at home, and move quickly towards not needing the daily Miracle Mascot on his desk anymore. Either way, the teacher has a behavior tracking chart that can be used at teacher or parent meetings, which takes approximately two seconds a day to record.

E). One last word on stickers. Some children need to see a visual representation of progress. Hearing "good job" from the teacher a few times a day is not enough for this child. They need a concrete view of exactly how good of a job they are doing. Every time a sticker is placed on their Miracle Mascot, it is a visual record of success. The "good job, I am proud of you" verbal praise coming from teacher and parent is reinforced by the visual sticker that stays in their eyesight all day. The child knows that he needs five to take the certificate home, so the excitement and sense of accomplishment builds as he reaches that goal on a daily basis. The daily Miracle Mascot on a child's desk also adds the dimension of administrators being able to come into a room and if the child is on task, the administrator gets the opportunity to put on a praise show, congratulate him, call mom or dad if he wishes, and slap his own special way-cool administration sticker on the Miracle Mascot. It is a way-cool sticker not because it actually looks any better than the teacher's sticker, but where it comes from. Getting praise from an administrator in a systematic way changes the dynamic between a chronically misbehaving child and the administrator and makes the child much easier to manage when they are having only a one sticker day. A while back I ran a behavioral program for a year for fifth graders who were not just light years below grade level but had severe enough behavior problems that they had been put out of other schools. We would make our own books in class and learn how to read them fluently. The reward for good behavior each day was for them to be able to march on down to the office and find an administrator to read their book out loud to. "Ladies and gentlemen, remember, I am not taking one single human being down to the office who would bring embarrassment to their family or myself, the teacher, by showing out in front of the principal. This is a privilege of the highest order. Your parents want to be proud of you and I wish to keep my job. I am not going to be working at a fast food restaurant tomorrow because you showed out today. Do we understand each other?" I would get a solemn nodding of heads as the children eagerly clutched their books to go get the praise from the people that matter the most in their world: the administrators. A hint to teachers everywhere: "You are absolutely not going to read to the principal today unless I am proud of the high quality effort that I know that you are capable of," is MUCH more effective in eliciting good behavior than, "If you don't sit down and be quiet I am going to take you down to the principal's office to be scolded for the ninetieth time." Every child has the innate desire to please adults. Some just don't know how to do it. They desperately need positive adult attention, but get it in the wrong way, which hacks the adult off, who showers the child with negative attention, which leaves a bigger craving for positive attention in the child and the cycle goes round and round. *The Miracle Mascot System allows the adults in the misbehaving child's life to break the cycle of attention seeking by building into the child's day lots of automatic positive adult attention.* Just give it to them. That's it. Lots of it. Pour it on. Some children don't get enough love in their life and are looking for it because love for a child is like water to a plant. I am not exaggerating. Check out the studies that have been done about children who were raised in loveless settings, such as the mass day care programs in the old Soviet Block. Love and adult approval are the two most powerful emotional needs in any child, anywhere. I don't care if the child lives in Brooklyn, Beijing, Soweto, or on a moon colony, they will all respond positively, over time, if they are loved and paid attention to in a positive way. Use the need for love and attention to shape a misbehaving child's actions into something positive and productive. This is the ideological rock on which the Miracle Mascot sits.

There you have it. Let's set about CREATING successful children. Our society depends on it. And it's fun.

CPSIA information can be obtained at www.ICGtesting.com
Printed in the USA
LVOW10s0837101014

408035LV00004B/10/P

9 781493 180516